"Are you saying that you're in love with me?"

Slowly Cordelia answered, "Yes, Marcus. I am."

"Really?" he grated. "Or is it my job you love? The glamour and fame attached to me?" He smiled sardonically. "Maybe you believe what you feel is love. But this isn't the first time it's happened. Women fall for famous men—actors, writers, racing drivers. Very nice for those who take advantage of it...."

"And you have?"

"On occasion."

Angrily she stared at him. "And is that all you were doing the other night, Marcus? Taking advantage of me?"

Books by Sally Wentworth

HARLEQUIN PRESENTS

HARLEQUIN ROMANCES

These books may be available at your local bookseller.

For a free catalog listing all titles currently available,
send your name and address to:

Harlequin Reader Service
P.O. Box 52040, Phoenix, AZ   85072-9988
Canadian address: Stratford, Ontario   N5A 6W2

SALLY WENTWORTH

the lion rock

Harlequin Books

TORONTO • NEW YORK • LONDON
AMSTERDAM • PARIS • SYDNEY • HAMBURG
STOCKHOLM • ATHENS • TOKYO • MILAN

Harlequin Presents first edition January 1984
ISBN 0-373-10662-9

Original hardcover edition published in 1983
by Mills & Boon Limited

CHAPTER ONE

THE view from the hotel balcony was breathtaking.
It looked out over a deep green valley rich with
strange and exotic trees, many of them tall
coconut palms that whispered in the light breeze.
Small white houses, roofed with woven palm
leaves, dotted the hillsides and grew thicker on the
lower ground where they clustered round the
ornate, pink-walled temple just visible through the
trees. The temple stood alongside the still green
waters of a lake built by an ancient king for his
queen, but where, on an island in the centre and
connected to the palace by an underground
passage, the king maintained his harem of
beautiful concubines. Across the lake the land rose
again, the greenery giving way to the misty
greyness of rock as the hills peaked against the
clear azure sky.

Cordelia Allingham breathed a long sigh of
pleasure, her soft blue eyes drinking in every detail
of the scene. The scent of flowers stole towards her
and for a fleeting moment she thought she found
something familiar in the fragrance, but then it
was gone, no matter how hard she tried to retrieve
the memory. The sun was hot on her bare arms,
even though it was quite late in the afternoon, and
she stepped back into the shadow of a gabled roof
overhung with dark red pantiles and sat down in a
rattan chair. She was tired from the long journey
but was much too enthralled by the scenery before
her to go and rest. And excited too, excited at the

thought of coming home, although even now she could hardly believe that she was really here in Sri Lanka, this beautiful island that hung like a jewelled earring from the mainland of India.

Or rather, back here, because she had been born in Sri Lanka just over twenty years ago. Only it had been called Ceylon then, and had been part of the British Commonwealth, not a republic as it was today. Not that she remembered a great deal of the country from her childhood, as she'd been sent back to boarding school in England when she was only seven and had spent all her holidays with an aunt, her mother's sister, who lived near Bath, because she was too young to travel so far alone. But then when Cordelia was about eleven her mother had joined her in England, leaving her father behind, and had never gone back.

Cordelia's memories of those years were vague, she had pushed them to the back of her mind as one tends to do with memories that hurt or are unpleasant; she only remembered vividly one incident, when her father had come home on leave from his job and there had been a terrible row because her mother refused to leave England and go back with him. He had always been a man of violent temper, and he had stormed out of the house. Neither of them saw him again until Cordelia's mother died when she was fifteen and he had turned up at the funeral. By then he was again living in England, working in a London office and hating every minute of it, his job as the manager of a huge tea estate in Sri Lanka lost when all the tea plantations were nationalised by the government of the new republic. So many years had passed without any contact that by then they were strangers, neither of them able to bridge the gap of age or apprehension. Her father had tried, clumsily, but Cordelia had been feeling too deeply the loss of her mother's love and support to do anything but coldly and instantly reject an offer of the same from anyone else. So they had gone their separate ways again with only the dutiful exchange of cards at Christmas to acknowledge any kind of relationship.

A noise from the next room along penetrated her thoughts and made her look at her watch. She'd been sitting dreaming on the balcony so long that it was time to change for dinner. Hastily she went back into her room and took off the jeans and shirt she'd worn to travel in from London. It had been a long journey: a fourteen-hour flight with refuelling stops in Zurich and Dubai, and then a two-and-a-half-hour drive from Colombo airport inland up into the hills to this hotel near the town of Kandy which they were to make their base. She had been worried about her father and had tried to persuade him to stay in Colombo overnight, but he had insisted on pushing on, saying that he wanted to get the worst of the travelling over and done with. Just as he had insisted that they have dinner as soon as the dining-room opened so that they could get a good night's sleep and make an early start in the morning.

Tucking her long fair hair into a shower cap, Cordelia turned on the taps of the rather ancient-looking shower and was pleasantly surprised when warm water came through. She stepped under it, wondering if her father was all right. Her father! She shook her head in puzzlement, amazed that she was really here with him. It had all happened so quickly. He had just suddenly turned up on the doorstep of the flat she shared with three other girls one day, and more or less demanded that she go with him on this trip. At first she hadn't recognised him; he seemed to have grown old since the last time she had seen him, his brown hair had turned grey and there were new lines on his face, his skin that had once had the tan of years spent in the hot sun, looked yellow and unhealthy. He had always been a big, hefty man, but now his flesh seemed to cling to bones that were too heavy for him so that his shoulders bent under the weight.

He said that he had been ill, that he wanted to go back to Sri Lanka to convalesce, but his doctor wouldn't let him go unless he had someone with him to take care of him.

Cordelia's first emotion had been one of pity when she saw how he had changed, but his brusque manner had almost immediately hardened her feelings. She had suggested he hire a trained nurse to take care of him, but this he had bluntly refused to do, saying that he was well enough, he only wanted someone to organise things for him, that he didn't really want or need a companion at all and it was only a sop to his doctor. Cordelia could well believe it and she had argued against going with him, pointing out that she had a job and couldn't take indefinite leave and that she was taking a course of evening classes. But he had bludgeoned down all her arguments with a wave of his clenched fist, a gesture she remembered from long ago. She could give up her job and he would pay all her expenses and her share of the rent of the flat while she was away. She could take her books with her and study while she was in Sri Lanka, and join the class again when she got back.

But even then she wouldn't have gone with him,

not just for his sake, and they had grown too far apart for her to feel any old-fashioned sense of duty towards him. No, she had agreed in the end only because she couldn't resist the opportunity to go back to the land of her birth, to see again in reality those dim memories of a land of sun and long white beaches, of brilliant flowers and endless seas.

Slipping on a short-sleeved cotton dress, Cordelia applied fresh make-up and tidied her hair. Seven-fifteen; she still had a quarter of an hour in hand. She knocked at her father's door but there was no reply; he must already have gone down. All the rooms on this storey of the hotel opened on to a stone-floored gallery with a white-painted balustrade. Going to the edge, Cordelia looked down and saw a pool with flamboyantly coloured fish darting among the pieces of lacy coral and the stems of lotus flowers, then she looked up and smiled delightedly; the well of the gallery had no roof, it was open to the evening sky.

She went on down the wide staircase and found her father sitting in the bar, a drink on the low table in front of him, a cigarette between his fingers. Cordelia crossed to sit in a chair opposite him.

'Would you like a drink?'

'Yes, please. A Bacardi and Coke.'

James Allingham raised a hand and beckoned imperiously to the bar waiter. He came over immediately; he was wearing a white jacket over a blue and black patterned sarong and he had plastic flip-flops on his feet. 'Yes, sir?' he asked with a wide smile on his brown face.

'A Bacardi and Coke and another gin and tonic,' her father said shortly.

'Does your doctor allow you to drink—and smoke?' Cordelia asked tentatively as the waiter hurried away.

'I'll do as I damn well like,' he answered curtly, his jaw thrusting forward obstinately.

Cordelia looked at him for a moment, then settled back in her seat. Well, if he wanted to make himself ill again what right had she got to interfere? And as she didn't particularly enjoy having her head bitten off every time she tried to show concern, then he could go ahead and do what he liked for all she cared.

The waiter came up with the drinks and Cordelia smiled and thanked him, getting a big smile in return. Her father didn't even bother to look up as his drink was put in front of him and the empty glass taken away. His attitude continued during dinner; Cordelia noticed that he was extremely short with the waiters, who were mostly young and very willing, although not speaking very fluent English. He never said please or thank you to them and got very impatient if they didn't understand what he wanted straightaway.

'The main language here is Sinhalese, isn't it?' Cordelia asked to fill the silence while they waited for their soup. He nodded and she went on, 'Didn't you learn to speak it while you were living here?'

'Yes, of course I did,'

'Why don't you use it, then?'

James Allingham gave a short, bitter laugh. 'These peasants are supposed to be running what they laughingly describe as a tourist hotel. If they want tourists to come here they must learn to speak their language. I certainly don't intend to pander to their laziness by helping them out.'

The soup came and Cordelia ate hers, wondering if her father had always been this bitter and bad-tempered or whether his illness had changed him. She could remember him being hot-tempered, but that was a far cry from this continuous sourness. If he had been like this all the time, then it was no wonder that her mother had left him; Cordelia could only marvel that she had stopped with him as long as she had. He must be getting on for sixty now, Cordelia reckoned; he hadn't married until his late thirties and his wife had been almost fifteen years younger.

There weren't many other people in the dining-room; it was August and the off-season for this part of the island, so they were served quickly and soon finished their meal. Cordelia would have liked to go for a walk to stretch her legs, but it was already dark outside and she didn't fancy going alone in case she got lost; the hotel had seemed to be situated among a maze of narrow, unmade-up roads when they had arrived, and there weren't any street lights. One glance at the lines of tiredness around her father's eyes decided her against asking him to go with her, and anyway, a few moments later he stood up and announced that he was going to turn in.

'I've already arranged for a car for tomorrow,' he informed her. 'You'll need to be down for breakfast at seven-thirty and we'll leave at eight.'

Anger at his high-handedness almost made her retort that she would get up when she damn well liked, but then she shrugged mentally; after all, he was paying for this trip, so she supposed he had a right to say when they would travel, but he could certainly be a bit more polite about it! She nodded briefly and rose to follow him upstairs. At his door they merely exchanged a brief goodnight and Cordelia went on to her own room. But she didn't immediately get ready for bed, instead she went to sit out on the balcony again and listened to the sounds of the night: to the dogs who had lain supine in the sun all day and only now came alive to fill the air with their howling, to the constant chirp of tree frogs, and the distant rattle of a train. And now that tantalising scent came back to her more strongly, a faint spicy muskiness, and at last the memory returned: it was the smell of Sri Lanka, the land of her birth, and the only thing that had stayed with her over the years she had been away. Suddenly her heart surged with emotion and she was filled with a sense of peace and satisfaction, the knowledge that she had come home.

The car her father had ordered was waiting for them outside the entrance of the hotel punctually next morning. It was a large black car which looked as if it had seen better days. Beside it stood a smartly dressed Sri Lankan driver.

'Good morning, sir. Good morning, madam.' He rushed to open the rear door for them.

'We don't need you,' James Allingham told him. 'I only ordered a car, not a driver.'

'Oh, but sir,' the man started to protest, 'to a stranger these roads can be very dangerous. It is better if I drive you.'

'I'm no stranger,' her father informed him tersely. He turned impatiently to Cordelia, who was looking at the two men uncertainly. 'Come on, get in the passenger seat.'

She tried to compromise. 'Why don't I drive?'

He laughed shortly. 'Not on these roads. You'd have an accident within the first mile.' When she still hesitated, he added brusquely, 'I drove myself around this island for over twenty years and I'm quite capable of doing it now!'

Cordelia realised that there was no point in arguing, and got into the front seat hoping that he was fit enough to drive. It would help if she knew what his illness had been but when she had asked he had just shrugged off the question.

'There isn't much point in my being here if you won't let me do anything,' she pointed out rather tartly.

James Allingham looked at her coldly for a moment, then started the car. Cordelia felt completely snubbed.

Their hotel gripped the steep hillside overlooking the town of Kandy, and they were soon caught up in the early morning traffic making its way into the centre of the town. Everyone drove on the left, the same as in England, but this seemed to be the only piece of organisation among the general chaos. The road was thronged not only with cars, but also with ancient Mercedes buses, painted red and grey, all of them with scrapes and torn metal along their sides, and all of them so crammed full of people that they bulged out of the doorway, hanging on by one hand or on to someone else who had a better hold. There were slow bullock carts loaded with fruit or vegetables for the market, literally hundreds of people on bicycles as well as a few motorbikes and the smart mini-coaches used for tourist excursions. Everyone drove on their horns, so that the air was filled with the shrill cacophony, but the crowds of pedestrians who overflowed the pavements on to the road seemed to take no notice at all, only moving out of the way at the very last moment.

Cordelia decided that they must have built in radar or something, and she sighed in relief as an old man moved out of the way when she'd been sure that they were going to run him down. Her father had been quite right, she realised; she would never have been confident to drive through this lot, but he seemed quite unperturbed, even had a slight grin of enjoyment on his face.

Beyond the town the traffic thinned out a little, although the roads grew progressively worse and she was bounced around in her seat as they drove over ridges and potholes. Her father still sounded the horn peremptorily whenever another vehicle or some people on foot got in the way, but Cordelia had time to take in the passing scenery: the paddy fields where women cut the rice by hand, the working elephants moving huge sawn tree-trunks, the tiny open-fronted shops in the villages that sold strange fruit and vegetables and yellow king-coconuts for thirsty travellers to drink.

She had brought her camera with her and would have liked to stop a dozen times to take photographs, but her father took little notice of the scenery and seemed intent to push on. After a couple of hours' driving the road began to rise, running in big hairpin bends among steep hills that were planted with thousands of low, evenly cut green bushes clinging to hillsides that looked too steep for anything but a mountain goat to walk on.

'There are the first of the tea plantations,' James Allingham told her.

'Is this where we used to live?'

'No, the old Braemar plantation is some miles farther on in the best soil area.'

Sri Lanka seemed to be full of people, even out here there were men walking barefoot along the

side of the road, and women washing themselves
or their clothes under one of the small waterfalls
that cascaded over the grey rocks, and there were
small children with bunches of exotic wild flowers
in their hands who tried to attract their attention
so that they would stop and buy the flowers from
them.

The road rose higher and the hairpins became
sharper until, at the top of one very steep hill, her
father pulled off the main road and stopped
outside a huge grey building that dominated the
landscape.

'Here we are,' he said. 'This is the Braemar tea
factory.'

He didn't get out of the car straight away, but
sat looking round, and Cordelia tactfully stayed
silent. Obviously the place was bringing back
memories for him, but she was disappointed to
find that she could remember nothing of the place.
After a few minutes he gave a sort of grunt of
dissatisfaction and got slowly out of the car,
Cordelia following. The day was really starting to
get hot, even so high up where a breeze came off
the hills. She was wearing only a sundress but
already she was beginning to feel the heat. There
was a sort of courtyard outside the factory with,
on the far side, a low, newish-looking building
with 'Tourist Reception' written on the door.
James Allingham grunted disgustedly when he saw
this and walked straight towards the entrance to
the factory, completely ignoring it.

As they approached the door, however, a girl in
a green sari came out of the tourist office and ran
after them. 'Please, you wish to see the factory? I
will take you.'

Her father turned and eyed the girl with thinly-veiled contempt. 'I don't need some girl to take me round. I know the workings of this place better than you ever will.'

The girl's smile stayed on her face. 'Oh, but sir, it is not allowed that you go alone. I must take you.'

He snorted angrily. 'Come, if you must, but I'll do my own tour.'

Taking a firm hold of Cordelia's elbow, he led her into the cool shade of the factory and started to tell her how the tea was processed, climbing up steep flights of stairs that were more like ladders, to the upper floors where the drying racks were and then down again to see the more mechanised part of the operation and finally to the white-tiled testing room where the different grades of tea were tasted. By this time he was puffing a bit and there were patches of colour on his cheeks.

Trying to keep any sign of concern out of her voice, Cordelia said carefully, 'Looking at that tea makes me feel thirsty; is there somewhere where we could try it?'

The guide had followed them all round, hovering in the background, and now she said, 'Oh, yes. We offer cups of tea to our visitors in the tourist centre. Or there is a place outside if you prefer it.'

'We'll take it outside.'

They walked out and sat under the shade of a circular, thatched-roof building that was open on all sides. It looked out over the deep valleys and steep hills of the tea plantations, the colour of the bushes giving the hills a uniform green appearance. Cordelia sat with the sun hot on her back and wished her father would stop going on about the lack of improvements that had taken place since

his time. 'They've hardly brought in any mech-
anisation,' he was saying disparagingly. 'They
could treble their rate of production and packing if
they used modern methods. Too many of the
processes are still done by hand.'

'How big did you say this island is—about the
size of Scotland?' Cordelia asked him.

'About that.'

'And there are over fifteen million people living
here?'

'Yes.'

'Then,' she pointed out reasonably, 'perhaps it's
better for them not to be mechanised. If they
brought in machines they would throw thousands
of people out of work and the state would have to
keep them out of the extra profit they made from
the tea factories. It's a Catch 22 type situation.'

James Allingham looked at her coldly. 'And
since when have you become an economics
expert?' he demanded sneeringly.

A flash of anger shone in Cordelia's eyes, but
she was prevented from making the sharp retort
that came to her lips by the return of the guide
with a tray with cups of tea of different grades for
them to try. The girl fussed over them, still polite
and smiling despite her father's rudeness. He asked
her if they still had the records of people who had
worked at the plantation and seemed more put out
than the answer warranted when the girl said that
they only kept the records for three years. When
they had tried the tea, which he pronounced as
'inferior quality rubbish', he turned to the girl and
told her that he wanted to see round the manager's
bungalow.

'But that is a private house,' the girl protested.

'Nevertheless I want to see it. I was the manager

of this place myself before it was stolen from the rightful owners by your government. I used to live in the manager's house and my daughter was born there. I want her to see it.'

'Oh, no, please,' Cordelia protested. 'It may not be convenient.'

'Then they'll have to make it convenient,' her father snapped. 'I didn't come all the way here to be fobbed off by some native girl!'

Cordelia flushed with embarrassment and walked away from him. If she hadn't she would really have let go and told him just what she thought of his boorish manners. The door of the tourist centre was open and she went in. There were some other people there, sitting around drinking the tea, enjoying their holiday. Cordelia was beginning to wish she'd never come. She bought a few packets of the best grade tea to take back as presents, but her mind wasn't really on it, she was just wondering how she was going to get through the rest of their visit here without losing her temper.

The next hour was as bad as Cordelia expected it to be. They had to wait some time until the girl came and said they could go to the bungalow, her father growing more impatient by the minute, and he ruined any enjoyment she might have found in seeing the house where she was born. The wife of the present manager, whose home and privacy he was invading, he treated as if she was some usurper who was trespassing in a house that still belonged to him. He pointed out to Cordelia things that had been added since his time and spoke loudly and disparagingly of the alterations. 'These people are little more than peasants,' he informed her. 'They don't know what civilised standards are.'

Cordelia bit her lip and somehow held on to her temper, knowing that to lose it in front of strangers would only make things worse. The manager's wife was obviously puzzled and upset by his attitude, but she remained unfailingly polite, even offering them more tea and cakes which James Allingham brusquely refused. They looked round the garden, which Cordelia thought was lovely, but in whose flowers and beautiful, exotic trees he could only find a poor comparison, and then, to her relief, they left. But, to add insult to rudeness, as they went out he gave the poor woman only a cursory word of thanks and dropped a twenty-rupee note on to a table as a tip. Cordelia hadn't remembered the bungalow, but she thought she would never forget the look on that woman's face as long as she lived.

She managed to control her feelings until they were back in the car and driving away, but then she turned to face her father and said furiously, 'How could you behave so rudely? Just because you happened to be the manager of that plantation once it doesn't give you the right to treat the people there now like dirt, does it? And to throw down money for that woman after you'd barged your way into her home—it was . . .' her anger almost choked her, 'it was disgusting!'

Her father glared at her. 'Who the hell do you think you're talking to? And just what do you think you know about these people? They're just one generation removed from peasants and they have to be kept in their place. And they never do anything unless it's for money. You'll soon find that out. They're a greedy, lazy rabble, the lot of them!'

'The ones I've met have been polite and friendly enough.' Cordelia started to argue back, but he turned on her and shouted her down. He started to get very red in the face and the car swerved wildly as he took a corner too fast and swung it back on to the road. A car coming the other way hooted furiously and Cordelia remembered that he'd been ill. Gripping her hands into tight fists, she forced herself to sit in silence and not answer back, her mouth pressed grimly shut, and eventually James Allingham calmed down a little, although he still drove too fast in angry defiance of her criticism.

They had lunch at the Hill Club in Nuwara Eliya. The town had been built during the British occupancy as a hill station and looked like any English town—it even had a golf course and a racecourse. The Hill Club was a large building of grey stone that looked rather like an English manor house in the Cotswolds except for the statues of lions on either side of the entrance portico and the elephant's foot umbrella stand in the hallway. They had a drink in the bar before going into the large, polished oak dining-room where lunch was served to them by very correct waiters in white jackets and sarongs. Cordelia stuck to food she recognised, but her father asked for curry, insisting on having it very hot. He drank a lot of beer to go with it, several times asking for his glass to be refilled.

Afterwards they had coffee, but James Allingham was soon on his feet again. 'I want to drive round the town before we go back,' he said eagerly.

Cordelia followed him willingly enough; he had seemed more at ease at the Hill Club, a place that he had frequented during his time in Sri Lanka and which had remained much the same. But the

changes that had taken place in the town brought
his anger flooding back.

'Look at that!' he pointed out furiously. 'They've
turned one of the best homes around into a damned
hotel!' And he complained about other places that
had been neglected. 'They've let the whole place go
to rack and ruin. I bet nobody's lifted a finger since
we were here to stand over them and tell them what
to do all the time.' He slammed his fist down angrily
on the steering wheel. 'They've even closed the
bloody racecourse!'

Abruptly he turned the car and started driving
fast out of the town. 'I'm getting out of this place!
I should never have come back here.'

They went back the same way as they had come,
along the road that climbed up into the hills and
snaked along in steep hairpin bends.

'Oh, look!' Cordelia exclaimed. 'Those two little
boys with the flowers are racing us by running
straight down the hillside while we go round by
the road.' She watched and laughed delightedly
when the two boys arrived panting on the lower
road and looked at them with expectant grins as
they drove up. Her father drove right by without
even glancing at them, but the boys plunged
gamely across the road and down the path while
the car went round the next hairpin. The boys
were there ahead of them again on the lower level,
both panting for breath. 'There they are. Stop a
minute so that I can give them something.'

But James Allingham drove straight on again.

'Why didn't you stop?' Cordelia asked in
surprise and disappointment.

'I'm not encouraging those kids. There are
enough of them begging from tourists and making
nuisances of themselves already.'

The two boys started to run down to the next stretch of road and Cordelia, her patience snapping, said tartly, 'I don't know why you wanted to come back here when you obviously hate the place and the people so much. Or is it that you're just a masochist?'

'Don't try and pin labels on me, girl,' her father returned angrily. 'Especially when you don't know what the hell you're talking about!'

'Then why did you come back? You obviously aren't enjoying yourself, and you're rude to the people even though they're very friendly and . . .'

'That's the trouble,' James Allingham shouted in sudden vehement anger. 'They're too bloody friendly! Always smiling at you and talking to you and making you feel that you want to get to know them. You have to keep them at a distance, do you hear me? You have to push them away before they get too close!'

He was shouting at her now and had gone red in the face. To Cordelia's horror he suddenly began to clutch at his collar, beads of sweat grew on his forehead and he started to make great gasping noises as if he couldn't get his breath.

'Dad!' Cordelia cried out in fear and horror as he held both hands to his chest and gave a great cry of agony, then he slumped forward, falling across the steering wheel.

'Dad! Dad!' She screamed in terror, realising that the car was running out of control. Desperately she grabbed the wheel, but her father's weight made it impossible to steer and he was too heavy for her to push out of the way. They were going downhill, approaching the next hairpin and the steep drop down the hillside. Acting by pure instinct, Cordelia grabbed the

handbrake and jerked it on. The car slowed but
didn't stop because her father's foot was still on
the accelerator. With a sob of despair, she threw
herself down and reached across to push his foot
off the pedal, then she put both hands on the
footbrake and rammed it down as hard as she
could go. The car slowed, came to a stop, and for
a wonderful moment she thought that they were
safe, but then it teetered and slid over the edge,
falling on its side as it careered down the hillside.

Curled up as she was on the floor, Cordelia
wasn't thrown about too much, she hung on to the
gear lever, but her left hip was banged repeatedly
against what was now the floor and once her arm
came up against something sharp and she cried out
in pain. Her father fell down across the seat and
was partly lying on top of her. His eyes were
closed and he seemed quite unconscious. For a
few paralysing minutes, as the car plunged on, and
Cordelia was crushed under his weight, she
thought that he was dead. Then, after what seemed
like an eternity, the car seemed to hit a harder
surface, it rocked and then came to a standstill.
Tentatively, almost forcing herself to do so, she
managed to free one arm and put her hand on her
father's chest. Faintly she felt it move, felt him
breathing.

The two little boys with the flowers were the
first to reach them. They climbed on the car and
wrenched open the door, talking at the tops of
their voices in a language she didn't understand.
They were too small to help, but soon they came
back with some men, workers on the tea estates. It
took four of them to lift her father out and
Cordelia got trodden on more than once as she
was still pinned underneath. When it was her turn

to be pulled out, she found that her legs wouldn't support her. She collapsed on to the grass and knelt there trembling. Looking around, she saw the great swathe that the car had cut through the undergrowth growing on the hillside until it had come to rest on a lower section of the road just before the hairpin. They had been lucky; she had managed to slow the car enough so that it just slid down instead of speeding over the edge and hurtling down from one level to the next all the way down the hill.

Quite a crowd had gathered round them now. A brightly painted lorry loaded with coconut fibre had stopped and the driver and his two passengers ran over and started shouting at the people who were standing round. Everyone was talking terribly loudly, waving their arms about and calling to others who seemed to appear from nowhere. They had laid her father on the grass and Cordelia crawled over to him. His face was grey and his breathing was very shallow. Several men and women were standing by him, but no one seemed to be *doing anything*.

She looked round wildly at the crowd of dark faces that stared at her so curiously. 'Please – somebody get an ambulance. Telephone for an ambulance!' Her plea came out on a high, hysterical note and for a moment the noise ceased as they all turned to stare at her. Then they all started talking volubly again, at her, at each other – and she couldn't understand a word.

'A doctor! You must get a doctor.' Cordelia staggered to her feet and only then became aware that her hip was terribly painful. Someone put out a hand to steady her, but she shook him off angrily. She pointed wildly at her father. 'He needs a doctor. Can't you understand? Where's the nearest telephone?'

But it was no use, they couldn't understand her, and even if they did, they had probably never used a telephone in their lives. She began to stagger along the road, reeling unsteadily, her head swimming, with some wild idea of walking to the nearest tea factory and using their phone to get help. Some men ran after her and caught hold of her, trying to pull her back, jabbering at her in Sinhalese. Tears of frustration ran down her cheeks. 'Leave me alone. I have to get help,' she muttered as she tried ineffectively to free herself.

Then she heard the sound of a car approaching and felt a great rush of hope as it came nearer and she saw a white man sitting in the front seat. It came to a stop and she somehow managed to shake off the hands that tried to restrain her and ran, limping, towards it. She reached it just as the door opened and a man stepped out. He was very tall and broad, and Cordelia's immediate impression of him was one of immeasurable strength. She almost fell against him and he caught hold of her, easily supporting her weight.

'What is it?' he asked sharply, his voice deep and wonderfully English.

'It's my father—he's hurt! The car crashed. Oh, help me, please help me!' she begged him, her eyes, dark with fear and panic, looking desperately into his.

The Englishman turned his head to snap out an order to the person he was with, then turned back to her. 'Don't worry,' he said reassuringly. 'I'll take care of him.'

She had been right about his strength, it was

there in every hard line of his face, in every intonation of his voice. Fortunately she recognised it and placed herself within it, letting the shock and fear take its toll as she fainted into his arms.

CHAPTER TWO

WHEN she came round, Cordelia found that she was being carried along, her head resting against a man's chest. For a moment she stayed still, taking in the masculine smell of tangy aftershave and the feel of the cool, clean cotton of his shirt beneath her cheek. She knew where she was and what had happened, knew that it must be the Englishman who was carrying her, but her head felt strangely giddy and heavy and it took her a moment or two before she could lift her eyelids and raise her head enough to see the strong, clean line of his jaw level with her eyes.

He must have felt her move, because he bent his head to look at her. His eyes were a very clear blue-grey under rather heavy lids.

'So you're back with us,' he remarked. 'Is your leg paining you very much?'

'No, no, it's all right.' She answered rather dazedly, not sure whether or not she'd complained about her leg. 'My—my father?' She tried to lift her head and look round.

'Easy.' The man's arms tightened. 'We've already got him in the car.' He came to a stop and set her gently on her feet by the open front door of his car. 'Shall I lift you in or can you manage it yourself? I've felt your legs and you don't appear to have broken anything, but I expect you're bruised pretty badly.'

'No, I can manage.' Cordelia got into the car, trying not very successfully to stifle a wince of pain from her hip. Her father was stretched across the back seat, his head supported by a slim, wiry native. He was still unconscious, but she could hear his breath coming in wheezing, loud pants as if something was restricting his chest.

The Englishman had gone round to the driver's side and got in beside her. Cordelia turned to him and said anxiously, 'Is he all right like that? Shouldn't we wait for an ambulance? I'm sure he'd be much more comfortable lying down.'

'I expect he would,' the stranger agreed rather wryly. 'Unfortunately there are no hospitals nearer than Nuwara Eliya, and it would take at least an hour for an ambulance to get here and then another hour back to the hospital. So I think it will be best if we go to my house instead. It's quite near, will only take us about ten minutes.'

He had started up the car while he had been speaking and drove gently along the rutted, twisting road. At the bottom of the hill, he turned off the main road into a narrower one for about a mile and then paused to sound the horn in front of a pair of tall gates which were almost immediately swung open from within by two men in native sarongs. The Englishman drove on between flowering shrubs and trees for another couple of hundred yards, then drew up outside a large, white-painted bungalow.

A native servant girl came out to meet him and was sent inside again to quickly prepare a bedroom. Cordelia got out, but could only keep out of the way and watch anxiously as they gently manoeuvred her father out of the car and carried him inside the house. She hobbled after them into a large, sunny sitting-room and sank into a chair, feeling completely useless, but quite sure that her father was in capable hands. She leant back in the seat, feeling suddenly sick and trembly. Her father had looked so white, so ill. Her hands began to shake and she closed her eyes tight to try and shut out the mental picture.

'Here, drink this.'

The Englishman was standing by her chair, holding out a glass. She hadn't heard him come in or pour out the drink.

'What is it?'

'Brandy.'

Slowly she reached out to take the glass, but her hand was shaking so much that he exclaimed and took her hand, holding it steady. His hand was very firm, his fingers closing over hers and holding them as she drank. The brandy made her cough and choke a little, but she felt a bit better afterwards.

'You're obviously not used to strong drink,' he remarked, taking back the empty glass. 'Now what are you trying to do?' he demanded as she began to pull herself to her feet.

'My father—I must go to him.'

She was pushed gently but firmly down again. 'He's in very good hands and there's nothing you can do. The doctor should be here any minute to look at him.'

'Doctor?'

'Yes, there's a medical team visiting one of the local tea plantations today and I've telephoned for the doctor. We were lucky that he happened to be in the neighbourhood . . .' He broke off at the sound of a car outside. 'This must be him now. Sit tight while I talk to him.'

He went away and Cordelia heard him greeting someone, then the voices faded as a door closed behind them. Leaning back in her chair, she looked round the large, comfortable room, which had one wall completely open to the garden and the cool breeze that came off the hills. The other walls were painted white, providing a stark background for the rich colours of several pictures and batik wall hangings. The furniture was rather ornate to Western eyes but was obviously of good quality and very comfortable. There was electricity too; there were lamps on some of the tables and a music centre on a unit against one wall. She had just begun to wonder who the owner was and what he was doing living in a remote part of Sri Lanka, when he came back into the room. Immediately she sat forward in the chair, looking at him with worried, apprehensive eyes.

He gave a quick, negative movement of his dark head. 'Nothing yet. It will probably take the doctor some time to examine him. He has a nurse with him, so I've been sent out of the way.' Hooking up a chair, he sat in it, took out a pack of cigarettes and offered her one.

Cordelia shook her head. 'No, thanks.' She shouldn't have done that, it made her head start to ache and she frowned in pain.

'Is your leg hurting you? Would you like to lie down?'

'No, I'll wait.' She remembered that he had said he had felt her leg to see if it was broken. He must have seen her limping. Cordelia looked at him and her cheeks felt hot suddenly at the thought of this stranger's hands on her.

Possibly he read something of her thoughts, because he said, 'Perhaps you'd like to tell me who you are—and how the accident happened. My name's Stone, by the way—Marcus Stone.'

For a second the name seemed to strike an elusive chord in her memory, but he was waiting for her to speak and she had no time to think about it. 'Ours is Allingham,' she supplied into the expectant silence. 'I'm Cordelia and my father is James. We're over here on holiday. We only arrived yesterday.' Her voice broke for a moment and Marcus Stone looked at her in quick concern, seemed about to speak, but she went on, 'My father used to work in Sri Lanka, on a tea plantation. He—he wanted to see it all again.' She hesitated, not even sure in her own mind that that was really why her father had come back. But what other reason could there be? Slowly she went on, 'We hired a car this morning to go to Nuwara Eliya. And then—and then on the way back he—he suddenly went all red in the face and collapsed over the wheel.' She shuddered, remembering.

'You say your father collapsed before the crash?'

His voice cut sharply through the horrific pictures in her mind, bringing her back to reality. She nodded dumbly.

'It may help the doctor to know that. I'll go and tell him.'

He was gone for longer this time and when he came back the doctor, a middle-aged Sri Lankan with thinning hair and a moustache, was with him.

'Miss—Allingham?' The doctor sat down on the chair Marcus Stone had vacated. 'Does your father have a heart condition?'

Cordelia shrugged helplessly. 'I'm afraid I don't know. You see, I haven't seen him for some time until quite recently. I know that he's been ill, but—well, he wouldn't tell me what had been wrong with him.'

Both men looked surprised at this statement. 'Could he have had a heart attack?'

'I'm sorry, I just don't know. I did ask him, but he just wouldn't tell me. He shrugged it off and said it hadn't been anything serious.'

'I see,' the doctor murmured, although he plainly didn't understand. Probably he thought it was just another example of foreign madness. 'Did you have a meal recently?'

'Why, yes,' Cordelia answered in surprise. 'At the Hill Club in Nuwara Eliya.'

'And I suppose you had curry?'

'My father did. I just had an omelette.'

'Did he ask for it very hot?'

'Yes, he insisted on it. He said they did the best curry on the island.'

The doctor snorted impatiently. 'A hot curry, the heat, driving along dangerous roads; it is no wonder he had a heart attack!'

'A heart attack?' Cordelia stared up at him in growing horror. 'Is he—is he . . .?'

'No, he's going to be all right,' Marcus Stone put in quickly before the doctor could answer. 'Evidently the attack was only a minor one, but he suffered some other injuries in the crash; he has severe concussion and has hurt his ankle.'

The doctor, rather put out at being forestalled, added in a severe voice, 'He will get well, slowly, if he keeps calm and does not get excited. But it will be several weeks before he will be well enough to travel back to England. And he is too ill to be moved to a hospital at the moment. He will have to stay here.'

Without hesitation, Marcus Stone said, 'That's no problem. We have plenty of room. Where are you staying?' he asked, turning to Cordelia.

'At the Ladyhill Hotel in Kandy, but . . .'

'Then I'll send someone to explain to them and pick up your things.'

'Oh, but we . . .'

'No buts,' he interrupted. 'You're staying here.'

'Good,' the doctor approved. 'I will send a nurse to sit with him tonight and I will call again tomorrow.'

'Oh, that won't be necessary. I can sit with him,' Cordelia told him.

'You are a nurse?'

'Well, no, but . . .'

'It is better to have a nurse.'

'Can I see him now?'

'I have given him something to make him sleep. You can see him when he wakes up. Now,' the doctor got up, 'I will look at you. Mr Stone tells me you, too, were hurt.'

'It's nothing. Just a few bruises.'

'But better I make sure. You have another room?' he asked, looking at Marcus Stone.

'Yes, of course.'

Seeing that she was outnumbered, Cordelia got to her feet, but her leg had stiffened while she was sitting down and she stumbled and gave an involuntary cry of pain as she went to put her weight on it. In one quick stride Marcus Stone was by her side, his arm supporting her.

'Ouch!' she gasped, clinging to his arm. She had to take a couple of deep breaths and then looked up at him and gave a shaky laugh. 'I seem to be making rather a habit of collapsing on to you. I'm sorry—but I'm very glad you're here,' she told him with sincere gratitude.

Looking up at him, she managed a smile through the pain and expected her rescuer to smile back at her, but his dark, straight brows flickered into a slight frown and a closed look came into his eyes. But then she was being helped into a pleasantly furnished bedroom with double doors leading on to a verandah overlooking the gardens at the side of the bungalow. There were two single beds with woven bedspreads. Marcus Stone helped her to the nearest, then turned and left, holding the door open for the nurse to come in as he did so.

The doctor confirmed that there was nothing seriously wrong, told her not to overdo things for a few days and gave her some pills for her headache. He told her to lie still and rest for a while, but Cordelia couldn't; the first stunned shock of the accident had worn off and she began to realise just how much trouble they were being to their rescuer. She could faintly hear the doctor talking to him now, the little doctor's voice high and foreign, Marcus Stone's deep and so reassuringly British. Marcus Stone—Cordelia was sure she'd heard that name before somewhere, but when she tried to think it made her headache worse. She was worried about her father and at the same time angry with him for not having told her he had a heart condition. If she'd known she could have been more forceful, have insisted that they hire a driver with the car. But it was too late now, the worst had already happened.

The voices in the corridor faded, she heard a car start up outside and drive away, and, five minutes later, it was followed by a second car. Cordelia moved restlessly on the pillow, worrying about what would happen to the car they'd hired, whether it was badly damaged. She sat up on the bed, realising that she should have made some arrangements for taking it to a garage, that she hadn't let the car hire firm know. Picking up her dress, she slipped it back on, then padded out on bare feet into the sitting-room.

Their host was standing by the window, looking out across the garden to the rising hills. He had a lighted cigarette between his fingers, but he wasn't smoking it, it had a long head of ash. He was very still, as if he was completely absorbed in something. Cordelia moved across to him, her bare feet quite silent on the tiled floor. She had thought that he had been intently watching some object outside, but when she came closer she saw that he was mentally absorbed, concentrating on something within himself.

For a while he didn't realise that she was there and she had the opportunity to really look at him, her mind unclouded now by fear for her father. His face in profile was strong and clean-cut with straight nose and high cheekbones. Perhaps a little too thin, the jaw a little too square to be called handsome, and, in repose, there were small lines at the corners of his mouth that gave it a bitter look. His hair was dark and thick, very clean and worn rather longer than was fashionable. His eyelashes, too, were thick and soft, but they were the only hint of softness about the face of Marcus Stone. But despite this, or perhaps because of it, Cordelia felt her senses quicken, his male magnetism attracting her and making her sharply conscious of her own femininity.

When, a few minutes later, he became aware of her presence, he didn't jump or anything, his eyes widened for a second and then he frowned and looked away, saw the ash on his cigarette and crushed it out in an ashtray with what looked to

Cordelia like unnecessary force. 'Can I get you something?' he asked abruptly.

'Well, no, but .... I'm sorry to bother you, Mr Stone, but I haven't done anything about that car we hired. I ought to let the owners know what's happened. And it will have to be moved ...'

'That's already been taken care of.' His eyes ran over her, apparently casual, but taking in every detail: her shoulder-length fair hair, her tall slimness, settled for a moment on her bare feet, then travelled up to her face to note her even features and the pallor from a long English winter spent inside an office, the hesitancy in her blue eyes. His own expression softened a little. 'I assure you there's nothing you have to see to or worry about. Everything's under control. I've sent a car to your hotel to explain what's happened and to collect your luggage. It should be back early this evening.'

'But the bill will need paying and ...'

He moved closer to her, caught hold of her agitated hands. 'Cordelia,' he said firmly, 'I've already told you to stop worrying. Now please go and rest; I'll see that you're called an hour before dinner, or immediately if your father wakes and asks for you.' His hands tightened for a brief second. 'Relax. There really isn't anything for you to do or to worry about.'

And in that moment Cordelia did stop worrying; it was as if she recognised and acknowledged his ability to take control, to efficiently organise and take care of himself and those under his protection. Perhaps it was the strength she felt in his hands, perhaps only her own present vulnerability and weakness, but her anxiety disappeared and she just felt terribly tired. She nodded and he let go her hands.

'Thank you for taking us in. And—and for everything you've done.' Her voice trembled. 'If you hadn't come along . . .'

'Nonsense,' Marcus's tone was brisk. 'It's the least I could do for a couple of compatriots.'

He offered to help her back to her room, but when Cordelia said that she could manage he didn't press it, just stood and watched her as she hobbled along.

She must have slept for a long time, because the sun was setting when she was wakened by a knock on the door and a voice she didn't recognise telling her that dinner would be in one hour. Her two suitcases stood neatly just inside the door and she wondered who at the hotel had repacked them for her. There was a bathroom opening off her room—and the water was hot! Cordelia lowered her stiff, bruised body into it and groaned softly. But it was a blissful kind of agony. She soaked for a good half hour and carefully towelled herself dry, afterwards examining herself in the full-length mirror on the door. Lord, she was going to have one hell of a bruise! Her left side, from her hip right down her thigh, was discoloured. She prodded it gingerly and found that it was also very tender. There were a few marks, too, on her left arm, but those she could hardly feel. She pouted into the mirror; it would look terrible with a bikini and some of it would probably show even under a one-piece.

Cordelia dressed carefully, wishing that she had more clothes with her, but at least she had brought one or two new outfits. She chose a soft, full white top with long sleeves which would hide the marks on her arms, and which had a matching flared skirt. She added white high-heeled sandals which accentuated the slimness of her ankles, and spent some time brushing her hair and doing her make-up. By the time she had finished the hour was almost gone, and she quickly picked up her bag and hurried into the sitting-room with only the slightest limp.

Marcus was pouring himself a drink, but he turned when he heard her heels on the tiled floor. He saw her and seemed to do a double-take, his eyebrows rising in surprise.

'Good evening. I hope I haven't kept you waiting.' Cordelia smiled up at him.

'Not at all. What would you like to drink?' He didn't smile back, after the first look of surprise his face had become quite expressionless.

'Do you have Bacardi and Coke?'

'Of course.'

He turned to pour the drink from a well-stocked cabinet, and she asked, 'Is my father still asleep?'

'I believe so.' Marcus handed her her glass. 'He did wake for a while earlier on, enough to be told that he was all right, and then he went to sleep again.'

'He didn't ask for me?'

Marcus shook his head. 'I expect he was still feeling woozy from the drug the doctor gave him.'

'Yes, I expect so.' Cordelia looked down at her drink, accepting this sop to her pride, then she abruptly changed her mind. Lifting her chin, she said sharply, 'You don't really have to try to protect my feelings, you know. I'm quite old enough to face the fact that he didn't ask for me. I don't suppose he even bothered to ask if I'd been hurt in the crash.'

Marcus looked at her, his eyes for a moment fully alert, concentrating on her face. 'Just how old is old enough?'

Frowning slightly, Cordelia replied, 'I'm twenty.'

'That's young to be so cynical.'

'I'm not being cynical, just realistic.' But even so she couldn't keep a slight trace of bitterness out of her voice.

'When I first saw you I thought you were younger, but now you look so . . .'

'Yes?' Cordelia queried when he hesitated.

'So different,' he finished.

But somehow she had a strange feeling that that wasn't what he'd been going to say at all.

A servant came with quiet feet and voice to say that dinner was ready, and Marcus led her into a smaller room opening off to the right of the sitting-room. This room, too, had its windows open to the cool of the night air so that the flame of the candles on the table flickered a little and cast shadows on the walls. Cordelia took her place opposite him at a round table that was just too large to be intimate, too small to be impersonal.

He made a few small-talk remarks while they were eating their soup and Cordelia guessed that he was being tactful; most people would have followed up her remark about her father and wanted to know why she was so sure he hadn't asked after her. She was already regretting her outburst and so was grateful for his tact, and she tried to keep up her end of the conversation by asking him if he had always lived in Sri Lanka.

'No, but I've been here for nearly two years now.'

'And is this your house? Are you settled here?'

Shaking his head, Marcus answered, 'No, I rent the house from a friend. He had to go and work in America for a couple of years but didn't want to give up this place. I wanted somewhere quiet to work on my—on a project I've undertaken, so it was an ideal arrangement.'

'So your friend will be coming home soon?' Cordelia remarked, wondering what kind of project needed two years to finish but too unsure of herself to ask.

'Within the next few months, I expect, but there's no hard and fast date. We're neither of us tied by time.'

'How marvellous,' Cordelia said wistfully, 'not to be governed by the clock all the time. Not to have to work from nine till five all the year except for three weeks' holiday in the summer and a week at Christmas. Just to go away for a couple of years, give or take a few months.'

An amused glint came into Marcus's blue-grey eyes. 'It isn't quite as simple as that.'

'Isn't it?'

But he didn't follow up the invitation, merely said, 'I take it you work in an office?'

'Yes, for a solicitor.'

'As a secretary?'

'Yes.'

'And you hate it?'

'No, not really.' She tilted her head as she considered the matter, making her hair fall forward against her chin. Absently she put up a hand to lift it away, the gold tendrils curling around her fingers. 'Or at least I didn't while I was there, but now I'm beginning to hate the thought of having to go back.' She laughed slightly. 'My first taste of travel has gone to my head, I suppose.'

He nodded. 'It happens. That's why thousands of young people are always working or travelling abroad. It's a kind of wanderlust that comes with young adulthood and has to be appeased before one can settle down.'

'Is that what you're doing?'

Marcus gave a short laugh. 'Hardly. I got that out of my system quite some time ago. No, I just came here to get away from——' he hesitated and changed what he was going to say, 'because the climate is so good in Sri Lanka and because I wanted peace and quiet in which to work.'

'And now we've come along to interrupt you,' Cordelia said with embarrassment in her voice. 'I'm sorry.'

'Nonsense,' Marcus denied brusquely. 'I'm glad that I was in a position to be able to help, and you're certainly not intruding. Please don't think that. You're welcome to stay until your father feels fit enough to travel. And there are plenty of servants to look after him.'

'But your work?' Cordelia asked uncertainly.

'As a matter of fact it's almost finished. Please don't worry about it.'

He said it in such a final tone that Cordelia took him at his word, sensing that he regretted having mentioned his desire for solitude. He immediately changed the topic of conversation by asking her what she thought of Sri Lanka.

'Well, I think it's wonderful, of course, but then I'm biased because I was born here.' His eyebrow lifted in surprise and she went on to tell him about the circumstances.

'So this was to be a nostalgia trip for your father?'

'Yes, I suppose so,' Cordelia agreed doubtfully. 'Although I've never really thought of him as the type who would go in for that sort of thing.' Not that she really knew with any certainty what type of person he was at all.

After dinner she went quietly into her father's room to watch him while the nurse had a meal. She sat in a chair by the side of his bed and looked at him, studied him more closely than she had ever done before. But there was little to tell from his hard profile, from the lines in his leathery face that came from too many years spent in the sun. Cordelia realised that she really knew very little about her father and only had the biased idea of his character that she had picked up over the years from her mother and her aunt, and which was naturally prejudiced against him. Not that anything had ever been said directly against him; it was more an opinion formed from overheard conversations, from remarks that had been cut off in mid-sentence when it was realised that she was in the vicinity. And, added to that, was his boorish behaviour of the last two days which had done nothing to make her alter her opinion, had even emphasised it.

As she watched him, James Allingham's eyelids flickered and he moved his head on the pillow. His eyes opened and Cordelia stood up and moved a little closer. For a few moments his eyes travelled bemusedly round the strange, dimly-lit room, then he became aware of someone with him. A flash of joy came into his face, eagerly he spoke a word she didn't understand, perhaps it was a name. Quickly she moved forward to the edge of the bed, leaned over him so that she was within the light. The joy died from his face and he said heavily, 'Oh, it's you.'

Somehow Cordelia stopped herself from turning on her heel and walking out of the room. Tight-

ipped, she managed to say, 'Yes, it's me. How do
ou feel?'

He snorted. 'Bloody awful! What—what
appened?' He tried to move painfully in the bed.
I—I can't seem to remember.'

'There was an accident,' Cordelia told him,
oldly, unemotionally. 'The car went off the road.'
But she didn't tell him about the heart attack; it
vas up to the doctor to tell him that if he thought
is patient well enough to know.

'Where are we? At a hotel?'

'No. We've been taken in by an Englishman.
This house is near where we crashed. The man's
ame is Marcus Stone. He . . .'

But already her father's eyes were closing again,
s if the effort of concentrating for even those few
ninutes had been too much for him. Cordelia's
oice faded and she stood staring down at him,
vondering just who he had thought was with him,
vhat had brought such joy for an instant to his
ace. The name he'd said hadn't been that of
nyone she knew; it certainly hadn't been her
nother's.

The nurse came back soon after and, in a
vhispered conversation, Cordelia told her that her
atient had wakened. The nurse nodded, obviously
erfectly capable of dealing with the invalid. She
vas quite young and much smaller than Cordelia,
ut then the Sri Lankans were a race of short
eople, not many of them came up to her height,
ut the nurse seemed to take caring for someone
vho was so much bigger than herself all in her
tride.

Cordelia went back to the sitting-room. Marcus
vasn't there, but from behind a closed door to the
eft she could hear the sound of a typewriter and

guessed that he was catching up on his work, s
she decided not to disturb him by going in to sa
goodnight. The room was still open to the nigh
the wooden shutters not yet closed, and sh
wandered out on to the verandah that ran al
round the house. The scents of the flowers fille
the air and she put up a hand to touch the delicat
trumpets of the mauve and white bougainville.
that grew up the supports and along the roof like ,
rich and colourful vine. There were some step
leading down to the garden and Cordelia wen
slowly down them, the moon lighting her way. Th
garden was quite large by English standards an
was walled all round, but it was planted with tree
that gave off the exotic, spicy smells of nutme
and sandalwood, and with flowering bushes o
hibiscus and frangipani.

Somehow the night seemed to heighten th
scents and Cordelia followed her nose, movin
from one bush to another, recognising cinnamon
cloves and, from way back in her childhood, th
camphor that reminded her of best clothes packe
away with mothballs to protect them.

Her slow progress through the garden ha
brought her opposite the room in which Marcu
was working, and a movement from inside mad
her look up. The windows in the room wer
closed, but there were no curtains. He had got u
to get a book from a shelf and now sat down agai
at the typewriter. It was very much a workin
room, the walls lined with shelves, mostly full o
books, and there were a couple of steel filin
cabinets under a big map that had been pinned t
the wall. He started typing again and Cordeli
smiled to herself; he was very much a pick-and
peck typist, was probably only using two fingers

Her own speeds were very fast and she was proud of them, but then her smile faded as she remembered that they were now more or less obsolete and she had had to train all over again on a word processor.

Idly she wondered what work Marcus did; she tried to see what the map on the wall was of, but it was too far away. It didn't look like Sri Lanka.

His desk was sideways on to the window, the light shining fully on him. He seemed to be typing from a sheaf of notes, pausing every now and again to think or to make an alteration. Once or twice he made a mistake in the typing and she could see and hear his annoyance as he impatiently x'ed out the error and retyped it. He paused to think again, got up and selected a book from one of the shelves, moved towards the window as he turned the pages. Cordelia watched him, feeling safe under her cover of darkness. He seemed too big for the room; he really needed one that he could pace up and down in while he sorted out his thoughts, but his long legs would only be able to take a few steps in the confines of that study.

As she watched him, still intent on the book in his hands, it came to Cordelia that he was a very attractive man—attractive to women, that was. There was something powerful and slightly arrogant about the set of his shoulders, the thrust of his chin. The sort of man who could handle and take charge of whatever came his way—much as he had taken charge of her and her father that very day. And she rather thought that he was quite capable of handling women, too. She shivered a little, but not from cold, and moved nearer the window, her dress mottled in the moonlight by the branches of a jasmine bush. There was something about Marcus Stone that she had never met in any other man before and which she found difficult to define; magnetism perhaps, or just a super-abundance of pure basic masculinity? Not the flashy, flauntingly virile kind, but controlled power, machismo kept well in hand.

Without warning, Marcus thrust the window open and stepped out on to the verandah. 'Who's there?' he demanded sharply.

'Cordelia.' She moved forward into the light as she identified herself. 'I was just taking a stroll round the garden.'

'I hope you sprayed yourself with insect repellent first, or you'll be covered in mosquito bites,' he remarked drily.

'Yes, I did.' Climbing the steps to the verandah, she said on a note of apology, 'Please don't let me keep you from your work.'

'It's all right; typing is the part I enjoy least.' He reached in his pocket for a cigarette and lit it. 'How was your father?'

'He woke up. I just told him that there'd been an accident; I thought it better not to tell him about his heart attack. What do you think?'

'You're probably right. Talk to Dr Matara about it in the morning.'

Cordelia was leaning against the upright supporting the verandah and he moved to her side, leaning down to balance his elbows on the rail.

'How long were you intending to stay in Sri Lanka?' he asked.

'There was no fixed time limit; my father wanted to stay here for several weeks.'

'Good, then you won't have any worries about rushing back to England.'

'No.'

They both fell silent, not the kind of silence in which one tries desperately to think of something to say, but a tacit, companionable silence in which they listened to the soft sounds of the night that broke the quiet stillness: the splashing of a nearby waterfall, the jarring cry of a nightbird diving on its prey. Marcus drew on his cigarette, the glow highlighting the hard clean lines of his face. His shoulder touched her arm and she gave an involuntary shiver.

Marcus straightened up. 'You're cold.'

'A—a little.' Cordelia's throat felt strangely tight so that she stammered over the words.

'Come inside. Perhaps the shock of the accident hasn't completely worn off yet.'

He steered her through the door into his study and Cordelia headed for the inner door, glancing round with interest as she passed through the room. 'I am feeling rather tired, despite the rest I had earlier on . . .' Her voice trailed away as she frowned at the map on the wall; it seemed to be of some inland area with foreign-sounding names, and there was a long, irregular line drawn along most of its length. Her eyes travelled over the titles of some of the books on the shelves that covered the left hand wall. Reaching the door, she started to say 'Goodnight,' stopped, and then turned to stare at him 'You're Marcus Stone!'

The grey-blue eyes looked amused. 'I know,' he agreed gravely.

'But—I mean—you're *the* Marcus Stone. The writer. You wrote that fantastic book about the Great Wall of China.'

'I'm glad you enjoyed it.'

'Oh, I *did*.' Cordelia's hand left the door knob and she stepped back into the room, her eyes sparkling with excitement and interest. 'You made it seem so alive. You made me long to go there and see it for myself.'

The amused look faded as he gave a quick smile of real pleasure. 'Thank you; you couldn't have said anything about it that I would have appreciated more.'

Cordelia grew suddenly shy. 'I'm sure you must have heard it a million times already.'

He laughed. 'Oh, not a million, I assure you.'

'I've read a couple of your other books,' she told him. 'I'd like to read them all, but there are always such long waiting lists for them at the library.'

'Perhaps you'd like to borrow one now,' he offered, the laughter still in his voice. 'I have copies of most of them here.'

'Thank you.' Cordelia selected a book and turned to him. 'Are you—are you working on a book about Sri Lanka?'

'No. This one's about another wall—the Berlin Wall.'

'I guess one wall led to another?' she quipped, her confidence coming back.

'Something like that.' His face changed, became withdrawn and introspective. 'Humanity has been building walls to keep people out since the beginning of civilisation.'

'Or to keep people in,' Cordelia added quietly.

His eyes flicked over her. 'As you say. There are too many walls, too many barriers.'

And yet, despite his protest, he had just built a small one himself, between the two of them, Cordelia thought. She softly said goodnight again, but Marcus didn't answer, merely nodded abstractedly, his gaze fixed on the map with its thick red wall like a line of blood, and she knew that his thoughts were whole continents away.

CHAPTER THREE

CORDELIA undressed quickly and got into bed, intending to read for half an hour, but even though she was looking forward to reading the book, she found that she just couldn't concentrate. She had never met a writer before, or anyone who was in the least famous, if it came to that, and the thought excited her. She wished now that she had asked him lots more questions, found out more about his work, but perhaps she could ask him another time; there should be lots of opportunities while she was staying in the same house. That was if he was willing to talk about it; although other people obviously found it intensely interesting, perhaps to writers it was just their job and they got bored when people asked them questions about it all the time.

Giving up any attempt to read, Cordelia closed the book and hugged it to her, too excited to go to sleep. The last two or three Marcus Stone books had all been best-sellers, and she had little doubt that the one on the Berlin Wall would be no exception. How marvellous to know about the book before it had even been published! Perhaps Marcus might even let her read the manuscript, she hoped dreamily, ambitiously. And perhaps he might not; her thoughts grew more prosaic, more down-to-earth. As an uninvited guest in his house it was really up to her to be as unobtrusive as possible, to keep out of his way so that he could get on with his work in uninterrupted solitude.

Cordelia didn't know much about how writers worked, but she imagined that they spent long hours alone with the phone off the hook and a 'do not disturb' sign on the door. But then she remembered that Marcus had said that the book was almost finished—and also that he disliked typing. Maybe there was a way in which she could get to read the manuscript, and perhaps at the same time repay their host in some small measure for his kindness. If she offered to type for him ... Her eyes sparkled and she gripped the book more tightly. She imagined herself sharing his workroom with him, seated at a smaller desk, typing, while he worked on something else. Perhaps she would ask him a question and he would come over, lean close to her as he explained. Perhaps his shoulder would touch her arm again as it had done tonight. Cordelia put down the book and turning off the light, lay in bed feeling hot and strangely aware of her whole body. It was as if every nerve end, every pore of her skin, was waiting and expectant. It felt like that for quite some time until at last she fell asleep.

The idea of offering to type for Marcus was so strong in her mind that it was the first thing she thought of when she woke the next morning. She showered and dressed quickly, putting on one of the new dresses that she had bought specially for this holiday, and adding careful make-up. A table had been laid for breakfast out on the verandah where there was a breathtaking view looking out over the green hills of the tea plantations. But this morning Cordelia had little attention to spare for the view. Marcus wasn't there, so she turned to the white-jacketed servant who pulled out a chair for her and asked him where his employer was.

'Mr Stone has gone out, madam.'

'Oh. Will he be gone long?' The disappointment was clear in her voice.

'I think he will be back soon. Please—how do you want your eggs?'

Cordelia chose scrambled. Happier now that she knew Marcus hadn't gone out for the whole day, she took in the view, noticing the small, bright patches of colour among the tea bushes where groups of women worked slowly along the rows, picking the tea leaves and putting them into the large baskets tied on their backs. She saw a lorry travelling along a road and wondered if it was the same road that she and father had used yesterday, but decided that it was too near, that it must only be a secondary road leading up to a tea factory. After she had eaten her breakfast, she amused herself by reading the local English language newspaper that the houseboy brought her while she drank another cup of coffee, but presently a movement among the bushes in the garden caught her eye and she saw Marcus walking up a path between the trees. Her heart gave a crazy kind of jerk of excitement and she sat forward eagerly, but then grew suddenly still. He wasn't alone. There was a girl with him—a petite, graceful native girl with large, dark eyes set in a clear dusky skin. As they came nearer Cordelia saw that the girl was beautiful. She also saw that she, too, was being scrutinised just as closely and that there was an openly hostile look on the other girl's face.

But then the look was gone as the girl lowered her eyes and demurely followed Marcus up the steps to the verandah.

'Good morning. How are you feeling today?'

'Fine, thank you.' Cordelia gave him a rather

forced smile, intensely curious about the silent girl beside him, but trying not to let it show.

'No ill effects from the accident?'

She shook her head. 'No, none.'

'Good. How's your father? Have you been in to see him yet?'

'No. I thought I'd leave it until after the doctor came. Aren't you going to join me?' she added when he made no move to sit down.

'I've already eaten.' The Sri Lankan girl was standing a little behind him, but now he put out a hand and drew her forward. 'By the way, this is Sugin. If you need anything just ask her and she'll take care of it for you.'

The girl he called Sugin put her hands together and bowed in the traditional, respectful manner. *'Ayou bowan.'*

'Ayou bowan,' Cordelia returned the greeting, and felt a small flash of satisfaction as the native girl's eyes flickered in surprise at her correct pronunciation.

Marcus said, 'If you'll excuse me, I have an appointment.'

He took his hand from where it had been resting casually and familiarly on the other girl's arm and moved to go in, but stopped when Cordelia exclaimed, 'Oh, but I wanted to speak to you. To ask you something.'

'Yes?' His left eyebrow rose enquiringly.

She hesitated, looking from him to Sugin uncertainly. 'I—er—perhaps I could see you when you get back?'

'Okay. I'll only be gone for an hour or so. Sugin will look after you.'

He raised his hand in a half salute of farewell and stepped briskly inside, leaving the two alone together. Sugin made no effort to speak, so Cordelia forced herself to say stiffly, 'I take it you work for Mr Stone?'

The native girl's eyelids flickeréd and she hesitated for a fraction of a second before saying, in a tone that Cordelia thought had a note of mockery in it, 'Yes, miss.'

'Well, there's nothing I want right now, thank you. You'd better—get on with your work.' She had almost said 'go about your duties' but thought how dated that sounded, then realised it must be a throwback from when she had lived in Sri Lanka before; in her mind she could still hear her mother's gentle but firm voice instructing the servants that they had employed all those years ago.

Sugin turned and walked away, making no attempt to give a respectful bow now that Marcus wasn't there.

Cordelia looked blindly down at the newspaper as she wondered about the girl's position in Marcus's household—in Marcus's life! Dimly she remembered having seen a girl waiting at the door when she had first arrived here, but she had been so shaken up at the time that she hadn't really taken much notice, could only recall the girl having been sent hurrying off to make up a bed for her father, but not having seen her after that.

Looking down the garden, Cordelia couldn't help thinking that it seemed rather odd for Sugin and Marcus to have come from that direction. It was possible, she supposed, for them to have been inspecting the garden or perhaps just taking a stroll while they talked over household concerns, but in that case they must have taken a long time about it, because she hadn't seen them go out.

Folding the paper, she gave a quick look round to make sure Sugin wasn't watching her, then got to her feet and went down the verandah steps into the garden, retracing the path that they had taken.

The garden was just as delightful to the eye during the daytime as it had been to her sense of smell last night, but Cordelia for once paid little heed to the beauty around her, walking quickly across the grass that grew between the bushes and trees until she came to the wall that surrounded the garden. It was quite a high wall with broken glass embedded in the top, whether to keep out animal or human predators Cordelia couldn't tell. The path curved round a tangled mass of bougainvillea bushes just near the wall, and behind them was a solid gate set into its thickness, with a key in the lock.

Cordelia tried to open the gate by pulling at the handle, but whoever had come through it last had locked it behind them. She turned the key and the gate opened easily and silently, its hinges well oiled. Beyond the gate the path continued through a field where a few tethered goats cropped at the sparse growth of grass, then through another, much smaller gate, in a low stone wall, into a track that ran in front of a few spaced-out native houses where barefooted children played in the dust. She didn't go out there, just stood looking for a while, taking it all in, then closed the gate and locked it again and slowly walked back through the garden. Probably it was a short cut for any of Marcus's servants who lived in the houses; it must save them a long walk if they could avoid going round by the road. Perhaps Marcus had been visiting someone in the houses and Sugin had walked back with him. Perhaps he had ... Oh, it could be anything!

Cordelia shook her head, angry with herself. She was just pulling ideas out of thin air. Anything rather than contemplate the more obvious conclusion. And after all, what was it to her if Marcus came *to* the house early in the morning with a young girl and admitted that he'd breakfasted elsewhere? After all, the man had been living here alone for nearly two years; it was hardly surprising if he'd formed a relationship of some sort, with someone. It was really none of her business and she wouldn't think about it again, Cordelia told herself determinedly, then thought about nothing else all morning.

A servant came to find her, telling her that Dr Matara had arrived. After examining her father again, he came to tell her that he was in a weak condition and it might be several weeks before he would be fit enough to make the long journey back to England.

'How long will it be before he'll be well enough to move to a hotel?' Cordelia asked, not quite sure now what answer she wanted to hear.

The doctor pursed his lips. 'It is difficult to say. Two weeks at least. I would prefer three to be on the safe side. The nearest hotels are at Nuwara Eliya, which will be better for him as it is not so hot as on the coast. But are you in a hurry to leave here? I thought it was already arranged with Mr Stone.'

'What was arranged with Mr Stone?' Marcus had returned without them hearing him and picked up the end of their conversation.

The doctor immediately detailed what had gone before and Marcus gave her a speculative look. 'Of course Mr Allingham can stay until he's well enough. Unless . . .' he turned towards her. 'Have you spoken to your father this morning?'

'No.' Cordelia shook her head.

'I see.' He held out his hand to Dr Matara. 'Thanks for coming. Shall we see you tomorrow?' The two men shook hands and Marcus shepherded him out. When he came back he paused for a minute, then said, 'I'm sorry if you find it boring here.'

'It isn't that,' Cordelia assured him uncomfortably. 'Of course I'm not bored. It's just that—well, I feel that we ought not to impose on your hospitality—your kindness.' She paused uncertainly. 'After all, we're complete strangers. We have no right to . . .'

'But we're all British and a long way from home,' Marcus interposed. 'Don't you think that gives you some claim?'

'No, not really,' Cordelia said honestly. 'At least, it shouldn't. My father should never have come here knowing that he had a weak heart.'

Marcus moved across the room and sat down in an easy chair. 'Maybe he had some definite reason for coming back. Something that had to be done despite his illness—or because of it.'

'What do you mean?' Cordelia sat in a chair nearby.

Marcus shrugged. 'Men often feel after an illness that they ought to put their affairs in order in case it happens again. Or they feel that they have to fulfil a lifetime dream before it's too late.' He paused to light a cigarette while Cordelia digested this, then added, 'Didn't he give you any reason for wanting to come back here?'

'He just said he wanted to see the island again and to convalesce after his illness.'

'That was all?'

'Yes.'

'Strange.' He blew out smoke and the air-conditioning drew it upwards in a twisting spiral. 'Was that what you wanted to talk to me about?'

'Oh. No.' His eyebrows rose enquiringly, but she hesitated before answering, all the confidence and sense of excited anticipation that had filled her last night lost in uncertainty now. 'It was just that—last night I heard you trying to type and . . .'

His left eyebrow rose steeply above the other. '*Trying* to type?'

'Well, yes. A trained typist can always tell when someone picks out one letter at a time.'

Marcus grinned. 'You're quite right; I'm no typist. Sorry, I interrupted you. What were you going to say?'

'I just wondered if, while I was here, I might help you by doing some typing for you. My speeds are quite good and I make very few mistakes.'

Her voice fell away as she surprised a sudden alert look on Marcus's face. Then he said abruptly, 'It's very kind of you, but you're here on holiday and have hardly seen anything of the place yet. You must take the car and get out and about, see all the tourist sites.'

Cordelia hesitated, rather taken aback. 'But I should *like* to work for you.'

'Why?' Again that penetrating look.

'Because . . .' She groped for reasons. 'Because I should like, in some small measure, to repay you for your kindness and . . .'

'I don't want any repayment,' he cut in shortly.

Her head came up. 'Well, want it or not, I should still like to do it,' she retorted in a tone of determined sharpness, and saw a gleam of amusement come into his eyes.

'And the other reason you were about to give me?' he demanded.

'What? Oh, well...' She flushed a little, then said on a wistful, almost confiding note, 'I would like to act as secretary for a real writer. To feel that I've had even such a small part in the production of a book.'

He smiled. 'Are you a book person, Cordelia?'

'Oh, yes! I can read anywhere.'

'Even in the bath?'

She laughed. 'Especially in the bath.'

He laughed in return and Cordelia's heart felt a surge of excitement again, all her doubts forgotten, and she knew an instant of pure happiness.

'All right, you've got yourself a job. I did have a woman who came in to type, but her husband was taken ill with malaria and she has to stay home and look after him, so I'll be more than glad to give up my two-fingered attempts. But you must still see something of the island,' he added firmly. 'This must be a holiday as well. Now,' he stood up, 'I expect you'd like to go and visit your father.'

'When shall I start work?' she asked enthusiastically.

Marcus laughed again and put a restraining hand on her arm as she got to her feet. 'Don't be so eager! You might find me a slavedriver.'

'Oh, I'm sure you wouldn't be,' she answered easily, and then felt her throat go suddenly dry as she wondered what it would be like if she was really his slave. 'Would you?' she added softly, raggedly.

But he had let go her arm and turned away, hadn't heard or noticed anything, fortunately. He held the door open for her and then went to his

study while she crossed to her father's room and
knocked on the door. The nurse gave her a smiling
welcome, but James Allingham, who was sitting
up in bed, propped up by pillows, had only a short
nod for her.

'Good morning, Father.' She made no attempt
to kiss him and even the title Father came uneasily
to her tongue. 'You look much better today.' This
got no answer, so she tried again. 'Is there
anything I can get you? Or do for you? Perhaps
you'd like me to read to you for a while?'

'There's nothing wrong with my eyes,' he told
her harshly. 'If I wanted to read I'm quite capable
of doing so.'

'Yes, of course,' Cordelia agreed coldly. She
waited a moment, then said, 'There's nothing you
want, then?'

He frowned. 'Our things we left at the hotel in
Kandy; I gather they've been brought here?'

'Yes.'

'Did you go and fetch them?'

'No. Mr Stone sent his driver for them.
Someone at the hotel must have packed them into
the cases. Why, is something missing?'

Ignoring the question, he said, 'Did you unpack
my case?'

'No. I unpacked my own. I'm not sure who
unpacked your things—I think it was the head
houseboy. Why?' she asked again.

Some tension seemed to go out of him and
James Allingham relaxed against the pillows. 'It's
no matter. Just wondered, that's all.'

Cordelia looked down at her father, trying to
guess just what it was he had in his luggage that he
didn't want her to see. A sharp rap sounded at the
door and as she was nearest she opened it.

Marcus said, 'I wonder if your father is feeling well enough for me to meet him yet?'

'Yes, of course.'

She stood back to let him in, then shut the door and introduced the two men. They seemed to size each other up while she was speaking, then James Illingham shook Marcus's hand in a grip that was still firm despite his weakness.

Marcus didn't stay long; he merely assured the invalid that he was welcome at the bungalow as long as he needed to stay, and that he had only to ask for anything he wanted. 'And when you're feeling better we must have a chat about what Sri Lanka was like in the old days,' Marcus added easily. 'Cordelia told me that you used to manage one of the tea plantations and that she was born there. It's a great shame that you won't be fit enough to take her round the island yourself, as you intended, but I'll try to make sure she sees something of the place.'

Her father gave an abstracted nod, obviously not caring what Cordelia saw or didn't see, which made Marcus frown, but then he seemed to pull himself together a little and said, 'It's really most kind of you. But you mustn't let Cordelia be a nuisance. She can quite easily go and stay at a hotel or a rest-house somewhere until I'm fit again, you know.'

Cordelia's face paled at his rudeness. Stiffly, she said to Marcus, 'Would you excuse me?' then turned and marched out of the room.

Marcus must have left almost immediately after, because he soon followed her out into the garden where she had gone to try and walk off her anger. He gave her a deceptively casual look, his writer's eyes taking everything in, noting her anger and the bewilderment behind it.

Falling into step beside her, he said, 'I know it's none of my business, but if it would help to talk about it . . .'

Cordelia would have loved to talk about it if she had known what to say. But how to explain her father's overt dislike, a relationship based on nothing more solid than a blood tie, a journey undertaken together for selfish reasons on both sides, a reason on her father's side that she didn't even know and was beginning to be afraid of. None of it made for pleasant hearing. Slowly she shook her head. 'It's nothing. Really.'

'Nothing? When your father makes it obvious he doesn't want your company and talks about you as if you weren't there?'

A bright flush of colour heightened her cheeks and she looked at him with dark, unhappy eyes. 'Please,' she said entreatingly.

Marcus continued to look at her frowningly for a moment, then abruptly began to tell her about his visit to China when he had been researching his book on the Great Wall. He talked for quite a while as they walked slowly round the garden and the tension gradually left her. Once he reached up to push a low branch of mauve bougainvillea out of the way and paused to break off a sweep of blooms and give it to her. He went on talking easily, not looking at her, giving her time to recover, until he glanced at his watch and then at her face and saw that she was absorbed in his story. 'Lunchtime, I think,' he said firmly. 'I'll tell you the rest while we're eating.'

After lunch he took her into his study and cleared a place for her at a side table. Cordelia was surprised to find that the typewriter was a modern electric one. 'Can you use it?' he asked her.

'Oh, yes. This wasn't the machine you were using last night, though, was it?'

'No, I have a portable I drag around everywhere with me. I get on better with that.' He brought a wad of typed A4 paper over. 'This is what I was working on; it's the third draft of the book. I've been over it and made a whole lot of alterations and amendments and I was retyping it chapter by chapter. But if you could take that over from me, it would be marvellous.'

Cordelia smiled. 'I think I can manage that.'

'Good girl,' he said warmly, so warmly that Cordelia started to glow inside. 'If you have any difficulties or there's anything you don't understand, just sing out.'

'The only problem will probably be that I'll get so interested I'll stop and read it.'

He grinned and went over to his own big desk where there was another pile of typed sheets and began to go slowly through them.

Cordelia tried to work quietly, afraid of disturbing him, but the electric typewriter made little noise and he was obviously used to it, for he wrote on steadily. She felt a great feeling of peace and contentment, working there with the sun pouring through the open windows into the quiet room. The book was absorbing and she had no real difficulty in deciphering his thick, black handwriting, although after a while she cheated and asked him to explain something. He came over at once but didn't bend over her, instead pulling the sheet of paper round at right angles so that he could read it, then explained what he'd meant and what he wanted to convey. Which wasn't quite what she'd hoped for but in no way spoilt the afternoon.

They stopped at about four-thirty and went out on the verandah to have afternoon tea served in delicate china cups, Marcus insisting that she try it the Sri Lankan way without any milk or sugar. 'The Sri Lankans think that the way the English drink tea is a downright crime,' he told her. 'They always drink the pure tea, none of your blended stuff—in fact they consider that to be little better than dust. And they never put in milk or sugar, just use stronger or weaker tea to their liking, although they occasionally indulge in a slice of lemon.'

He passed her a cup and Cordelia sipped experimentally, then pulled a face. 'I think my insides must have got used to the English dust! I don't think I could ever get to like this.'

'Try again,' he encouraged her. 'It grows on you after a while.'

She laughed and bent to obey him, but stopped with the cup halfway to her lips as Sugin came out on to the verandah. Without waiting for an invitation she seated herself at the tea-table. Something flickered at the back of Marcus's eyes, then they were hooded again as he poured tea into a third cup and handed it to the native girl. She sipped delicately and then, as if he had asked a silent question, nodded and said, 'Yes, that is how I like it.'

Marcus turned to Cordelia and said smoothly, 'You must get Sugin to dance for you one evening. The Sri Lankans have their own folk dances and Sugin is very good. She sometimes appears with the Kandyan folk dancers who perform for tourists.'

'How interesting,' Cordelia remarked stiltedly, and asked Sugin how long she had been dancing.

while all the time wondering if that was where Marcus had met her. Had he gone like all the tourists to see the dancers and picked Sugin out, brought her back here to be—to be his mistress?

'For many years,' the native girl answered. 'You must start when you are a very young child to learn all the movements, all the dances. The dances are very precise and it takes much skill and gracefulness to become an expert.' The words were said in a polite, almost toneless voice, but were accompanied with a little curl of the lip that clearly told Cordelia that she would be far too gauche and clumsy ever to achieve such perfection.

Setting down her cup, Cordelia stood up and said, 'I'm afraid I'll never get a taste for this. If you'll excuse me, I think I'll go and finish that chapter I was working on.'

'There's no need,' Marcus assured her. 'Tomorrow will do.'

'But I'd like to finish it.' She smiled at him and gave a brief nod to Sugin, then left them alone together. But back in the study she didn't start typing again immediately; instead she absently picked up the spray of bougainvillea that Marcus had picked for her earlier and which she had put into a little pot of water on her desk. She looked at it absently, smoothing her finger over the soft petals, remembering how much she had enjoyed working with him, how right it had felt, and how everything had changed the minute Sugin showed up. Cordelia wasn't used to sophisticated, good-looking men of the world and she realised that she found Marcus exciting and attractive, and that he was famous too only added gilt to the gingerbread. It was a heady kind of excitement, one that she didn't have much idea how to cope with, but the presence of Sugin brought her down to earth with a thud again every time the girl made her quiet but disturbing appearance. Cordelia tried to think rationally, telling herself that Marcus was merely being kind, that he had no interest in her as a woman at all, only as someone who was in trouble and whom he had been able to help. But that, unfortunately, didn't stop her feeling attracted to him. She sighed and sternly told herself off; much better for you, my girl, if you just treat him as your host and temporary boss. Resolutely she began to type, but presently the sound of voices raised in laughter reached her through the open window; Marcus's deep and amused, Sugin's light, but to Cordelia's ears unnecessarily loud, as if the native girl wanted her to hear. Cordelia's flying fingers grew still, paused, then went on more slowly.

A little later she heard a footstep on the verandah and turned her head to see. Marcus stood framed in the window. The sun was setting and his tall, strong body was outlined against the brilliant red and gold of the sky. He put out an arm to lean against the wooden frame and said, 'I won't be in to dinner tonight, Cordelia. The government are building a big dam in the hills and there are a lot of Europeans working on the project. They've formed an Expatriates Club and I usually go up there a couple of times a week. I could ask Sugin to stay with you if you'd rather not be by yourself.'

'No.' Cordelia stood up abruptly.

'All right. Pack up working now. It's getting dark and you'll strain your eyes.'

He moved a few steps into the room, came close to her, but she couldn't see his face very clearly because he stood in front of the glowing sky.

Impulsively she asked, 'Who is Sugin?' and stared up at him, waiting for an answer.

'Sugin?' Marcus gave her one of his quick, searching looks, then said slowly, 'She came with the bungalow.'

So what was she supposed to make of that? Before she could say anything further, he casually put a hand on her shoulder and said, 'I'm putting the car and an English-speaking driver at your disposal tomorrow. Work out tonight where you'd like him to take you. There's the ancient Buddhist city of Anuradhapura, or Sigiriya, which has the most breathtaking views if you're brave enough to climb to the top. I'll leave you out some maps so that you can study them more closely.'

'Thank you.' Hesitatingly she added, 'Will you—be able to come with me?'

His hand was still on her shoulder and she seemed to feel him hesitate for a second, then he removed it and shook his head. 'I'm sorry, but I want to get on with the book tomorrow.'

'Then I'll stay and help you,' Cordelia responded instantly.

Again he shook his head. 'Certainly not! This is supposed to be your holiday. You must go out tomorrow and perhaps help me again the day after.'

His tone was firm, decisive, and Cordelia realised she couldn't argue against it. 'All right. Thank you.'

'Good. I probably won't be back until pretty late tonight, so I'll see you tomorrow. Give my apologies to your father, will you?'

He raised a hand in salute and left Cordelia to

tidy the papers she had been working on, feeling strangely dejected at the thought of a long evening alone, but at least being alone was infinitely better than being with Sugin for several hours.

After eating her solitary meal, she went in to see her father and found him sitting up in bed reading. There was a little more colour in his sallow cheeks and he seemed better, though still as disinclined to have her around. Cordelia wondered rather bitterly why he had bothered to bring her to Sri Lanka at all when it was so obvious that he had no time for her. He would have done better to have paid a nurse to keep him company and look after him.

Going into the lounge, she curled up in an armchair with the book that Marcus had lent her. It was one of his earlier books, a novel, for he wrote both with equal skill, and she was soon completely absorbed, lost to the reality of the world around her, the book holding her so that she was unaware of the passing of time. The houseboy came quietly into the room and set a drink down on the small table beside her, but Cordelia hardly noticed, although her hand went out and she absently sipped the drink. The house grew quiet as the servants went home to bed, but she went on reading, unable to put the book down.

It was almost three in the morning before Marcus came home and, noticing the strip of light under the sitting-room door, went to investigate and found her still sitting in the pool of light thrown by a standard lamp and just a few pages of the book left to read. Cordelia wasn't aware of his arrival, and he had time to reach her side and look at the title of the book before she gave a gasp of fright as she realised that someone was there.

'Oh, it's you! You made me jump.'

'Do you know what the time is?'

'Why?' She glanced at her watch. 'Heavens, is it as late as that?'

'You ought to be in bed.'

'I only have this chapter to finish.'

'Leave it till the morning,' he ordered.

'Are you crazy? I wouldn't be able to sleep for wondering what happened at the end. Go away so that I can finish it in peace,' she ordered in her turn, and quite as firmly.

Marcus chuckled, went over to the drinks cabinet and poured liquid from various bottles into a tall glass that he stirred with a long spoon. Then he sat in a chair opposite and watched her silently while Cordelia read on. At last she turned the final page, closed the book and gave a deep sigh of sheer contentment. Again becoming aware of him, Cordelia looked at Marcus with awe in her blue eyes and said almost reverently, 'That was wonderful—one of the best books I've ever read. Oh, *how* I wish I could write like that!'

'Have you ever tried?'

She shook her head. 'I know I couldn't.'

'You don't know what you can do until you try.'

'I know I couldn't do that. How did you start writing?' she asked curiously.

He stood up, setting down his empty glass. 'This is no time to start going into my life story—even if I wanted to,' he remarked drily. Coming across, he put his hands on her arms and pulled her to her feet. 'Go to bed. You'll be . . .' He broke off as she swayed, her legs having gone numb from being tucked under her for so long. 'Careful!' He caught hold of her and held her.

'My legs have gone to sleep.' Cordelia clung to the lapels of the light jacket he was wearing. There was the tang of tobacco and woody aftershave about his clothes. She moved to steady herself and one hand slipped inside his jacket and she could feel his heart beating under her palm. His body felt very hard, very hot. Slowly she raised her eyes and found him looking down at her, his blue-grey eyes glinting in the shadows thrown by the lamp. A queer breathless feeling filled her throat, her chest. She said, 'Marcus?' in an unsteady, strangled tone, and her arms slid up around his neck almost of their own volition. For a moment he continued to gaze down at her, then his arms tightened, pulling her roughly against him, and his lips came down to find hers, fastening on them compulsively, almost like a man who had been hungry for love for a long time. Cordelia's senses reeled, her lips parting before the importunity of his mouth. For a moment she was suspended in delight, enthralled by the warmth of his lips, but then a great surge of desire filled her and she began to return his kiss, her body intimately close to his as she surrendered to his embrace.

She didn't know how long it went on for, but it was much, much too soon when Marcus's lips left hers and he raised his head and loosened his hold. She stayed where she was with her arms around his neck, her lips parted sensuously, her eyes half closed in desire. When he didn't kiss her again she moved against him provocatively, but to her chagrin he only gave a low, amused chuckle and flicked a casual finger against her chin.

'Come on, young lady, it's time for all good little girls to be in bed.'

Cordelia recognised the mocking tone in his

voice and knew that he wouldn't kiss her again, that there had been nothing serious in it, but she decided to tease him a little, so she kept her arms round his neck and said with a sexy pout, 'Is that a proposition, Mr Stone?'

He laughed. 'Minx! Are you going to go to bed or do I have to pick you up and carry you?'

'Mmm, now there's no doubt about it; *that* really was a proposition.'

'Girls who don't obey me,' he told her, 'run the risk of being put across my knee and given a spanking.'

'Wow!' Cordelia's eyes opened very wide. 'Real he-man stuff, huh? This is getting more interesting by the minute!'

His eyes laughed down at hers in genuine amusement. Reaching up, he pulled down her arms and held her a little away from him. 'I wonder what you'd do if I really propositioned you,' he said jokingly, but with just a hint of seriousness in the question.

Cordelia felt her chest tighten again as she remembered his kiss. 'I don't know,' she said thickly. 'Why don't you try it some time?'

His eyes searched her face, but he was teasing again as he said lightly, 'Maybe I will—some time.'

Quickly she looked away, then put a hand up to cover a fake yawn. 'You're right, I am tired. Goodnight, Marcus.'

'Goodnight.'

Crossing to the door, she paused a moment to look back at him. Their eyes met briefly, then Marcus deliberately turned to switch off the lamp.

Cordelia undressed as quietly as she could, afraid of waking her father, whose room was nearby. Slipping into bed, she lay awake, her fair hair spread across the whiteness of the pillow. On any ordinary night she would have thought about the book she had just finished, or planned her sightseeing programme for the next day, but tonight was no ordinary night; tonight she had been kissed by Marcus Stone, and she could think of nothing else. Cordelia wasn't what might be called inexperienced; she wasn't exactly ugly and she had been kissed by many boy-friends during her twenty years, some of whom had been fairly hot stuff. But somehow they all seemed to fade into insignificance compared to what had been merely a casual kiss from Marcus. And that it had been casual on his part she was quite sure. She had let him know that she wanted to be kissed and he had obliged. It was as simple as that. End of story—except that that one kiss had been so devastating that Cordelia had wanted it to go on and on, to grow more passionate, to lead to . . .

Her body grew hot all over and she pushed aside the blanket, thin though it was. If that was only a casual kiss, what would he be like when he really meant it? The thought made her gasp and she turned restlessly on the pillow. She was being a fool. He obviously had the girl Sugin to take care of all his sexual needs, although somehow Cordelia didn't think that there were any strong emotional ties involved, not on Marcus's side in any case. Sugin was clearly possessive about him and didn't like having anyone around who might be in danger of becoming a rival—she had made that very obvious with her resentment of Cordelia. But as to whether either of them were in love . . . Perhaps if they'd been lovers for two years their feelings for each other wouldn't be so open. It was hard to tell, and a problem Cordelia had never had

o face before. Moodily she turned over and let
herself remember instead the feel of his lips on
hers. Her fingers gripped the pillow tightly. No
one had ever kissed her like that before. No one.
And she would see him tomorrow. It would soon
be tomorrow.

But the next day she hardly saw him at all. As
was to be expected, she woke late and found that
Marcus had already eaten and gone into his study,
and as soon as she sat down at the table, his
English-speaking driver came to ask her where she
wanted to visit. Cordelia had completely forgotten
that she was supposed to be spending the day
sightseeing and would much rather have spent it
working alongside Marcus, but he had already
refused her services once and she had the sense not
to insist. The last thing she wanted was for him to
think that she was chasing him. So she picked out
two or three places at random and the driver went
off to plan the route. When she had eaten,
Cordelia collected her bag and camera, said
goodbye to her father, and hesitated outside
Marcus's door, then decisively pushed it open.

'I just looked in to say goodbye,' she said
brightly, but he was sitting at his desk and hardly
looked up.

' 'Bye. Have a good day.'

'No shopping or anything you want done while
have the car?'

He looked at her then, a slightly surprised quirk
in his eyebrows. 'No, nothing.'

'Okay. See you at dinner, then.'

But his eyes were already on his work again, and
he shut the door feeling rather foolish.

The car was air-conditioned, but it was a hot
day and the roads were so bad that Cordelia told

the driver to stop in Kandy so that they coul
go into a restaurant and have a drink. Sh
looked across the lake to the island where th
king had been entertained by his concubines an
thought of all that had happened since she ha
last seen it; then she had been looking forwar
to no more than seeing again the country of he
birth, now she was to spend an indefinite time i
the house of a man she found infinitely masculir
and attractive and whose kisses excited her a
never before. She suddenly jumped to her fee
taking her driver by surprise, eager to get th
day's sightseeing over so that she could get bac
to the bungalow.

The driver made a conscientious guide, helpin
her up the steep, rock-faced hill to the temple c
Dambulla that had begun as a natural cave in th
rock and been patiently extended in ancient time
until now it was big enough to hold dozens c
statues of Buddha, with the walls and roof covere
in paintings which all had some religious signif
cance and which the driver carefully explaine(
holding a torch high above his head so that sh
could see. After the semi-darkness of the cave
hurt her eyes to come out into the full glare of th
noon sun, but there were a few trees where tam
monkeys played and did tricks for the titbits c
food the visitors gave them. They went down th
hill more slowly and Cordelia paused to give son
coins to the most badly disabled of the begga:
who sat on the rock in the open sun, their hanc
held out like the heads of cobras, waving in fror
of her. There were beggars everywhere, of cours
not always disabled, nearly always children c
poor people who saw a tourist and thought the
would try their luck. More often than not th

children would ask for school pens, although they were always provided with them at school. There seemed to be far more of them than she remembered, but perhaps as a child she had just accepted them and had taken little notice. The driver told her that every so often the government rounded all the beggars up and took them off to beggar colonies.

From Dambulla they drove across country to Anuradhapura, a large city built by the Buddhists in the fourth century B.C., stopping at a hotel for lunch on the way. So by the time they got there it was incredibly hot and Cordelia would have been content to drive around the city and stay in the coolness of the car, but her driver, Daya, insisted that they get out to examine every place of interest and explained everything and answered all her questions so conscientiously that she didn't have the heart to refuse. So she looked at the ruins of palaces and monasteries, at ritual baths and excavations, at huge dagobas, or temples, dome-shaped and topped by ornate steeples; she saw them as overgrown ruins, ravaged by centuries of time and weather; in the process of restoration with each brick being carefully replaced; and then restored as they had been originally, painted white and glistening in the hot sun.

Personally she preferred the mellow ruins, but Daya proudly insisted on taking her all round the restored temple. It was so hot that the heat rose in hazy waves off the concrete. At Buddhist shrines you have to take off your shoes and walk barefoot. Most Sri Lankans went barefoot all the time anyway, so their feet were hardened, but Cordelia found the sun-baked concrete so hot that she could hardly bear it and scuttled on tiptoe into even the smallest patch of shade whenever she could find one.

'We go now to see the sacred bo-tree,' Daya informed her, adding encouragingly as he saw her wilting, 'You like this very much. Very holy place. All pilgrims go there.'

Resignedly Cordelia got back into the car for another short, dusty drive and then got out again, took off her shoes and hat and listened to Daya's lecture on how the tree, that looked no different from any other as far as she could see, was an offshoot of the very tree under which Buddha achieved his enlightenment and which was over two thousand years old. Now it was housed inside a sanctuary and protected by railings topped with gold spikes. At its foot many pilgrims knelt, their heads touching the ground, while others filled little metal cups with oil and lit them, much as Roman Catholics lit candles in a church. Against one wall was a framework hung with hundreds of gaily-coloured pieces of cloth which Daya told her had been tied on to it as tokens of sacred vows that the pilgrims had made here. It was very noisy; in the distance they could hear the sound of a service being taken over a loudspeaker, there was the sort of muttering rise and fall of voices of people praying as well as the ordinary noises of the people coming and going around them. But somehow despite all this, and as different as it was from the reverential atmosphere of an English church, Cordelia felt that here, in this noisy little square, was the heart of a living religion, far more so than the grandly restored dagobas and their huge statues of painted Buddhas.

Afterwards Daya drove her to the local rest-house, built by the British to house intrepid tourists of a much earlier age. Cordelia relaxed under the elegant white colonnades and watched the monkeys who lived in the tree-shaded grounds as she sipped a very welcome drink in a tall, frosted glass. She wondered if her father would have brought her here and how he would have described the sites of Anuradhapura to her—not very sympathetically, she decided with a small grimace, and wasn't altogether sorry that he wasn't able to come with her. But this inevitably led her to wonder what it would have been like with Marcus with his writer's eye for detail and his alert mind that could seize on the interesting or unusual. Cordelia wished very much that he had been with her, that they had shared the day together. Sightseeing really wasn't much fun unless you had someone to share it with, preferably someone you cared about.

So did that mean that she cared about Marcus? Cordelia settled back in her chair and thought about it. She certainly found him fun to be with and he had a magnetic personality that was impossible to resist, and he was so sure of himself, so self-confident. Cordelia hadn't met many men who were so positive, so vigorously masculine before, and it was hardly any wonder that he had made such an impression on her. But to care about him? When she'd only known him for a couple of days? Surely that wasn't possible? It must just be the thrill of meeting and working with someone so famous that had made her feel like this, she decided.

She was still quite sure of this on the long journey home, as she sat in the back of the car and watched the lamps being lit in the houses and tiny shops as the day gave way to dusk. Soon it grew dark and Daya had to drive more slowly, sound his horn even more often to clear the road ahead. The miles seemed to drag by as Cordelia grew more and more impatient to get home to see Marcus, to tell him about her day. She tried to remember things she'd seen that might interest or amuse him, telling herself that she was only eager to tell him because he was a writer and might be able to use them. At last they reached the hill leading down to the bungalow and she saw its welcoming lights shining out across the valley. She sat forward, her heart beating faster than it should, and somehow managed to thank Daya properly before turning to run into the bungalow to find Marcus.

But only Sugin was waiting for her inside, a Sugin who took in her eager face and searching eyes and said cruelly, 'Marcus has gone out. He decided not to wait for you. You will have to eat alone—again.' With a slight but insulting emphasis on the 'again'.

And Cordelia knew then that, even though she had only known him for a short time, she did care. She cared very much.

CHAPTER FOUR

IT was very late. Glancing at her watch, Cordelia saw that it was nearly nine-thirty. It had taken them over four hours to cover the bad, crowded roads from Anuradhapura.

'You have eaten on the way?' Sugin asked her.

Cordelia shook her head. 'No, not since lunch.'

'Then I will tell them to cook you something.'

'Please don't bother, I'm quite capable of . . .'

But the other girl had already gone out into the hall and was shouting something in Sinhalese to the people in the kitchen. After a few moments she came back and said, 'I have told the cook to make you some soup and an omelette. Then he and the others can go home.' She said it as if the whole staff had been kept waiting for hours.

'Thank you,' Cordelia said stiffly. 'I will be ready to eat it in half an hour.' Going into her room, she showered and changed, finding it blissful to be cool and clean again after the hot sweatiness of the long day. Automatically she brushed her hair and put on fresh make-up, although there was no impetus to do so when Marcus wasn't going to be there. She expected Sugin to have gone when she returned to the sitting-room, but the other girl was still there and followed her into the dining-room, calmly seating herself in the place where Marcus usually sat.

'You enjoyed visiting the ancient places in Sri Lanka?' Sugin asked, her tone not in the least interested or friendly.

'Very much, thank you,' Cordelia answered after she had smilingly thanked the servant who brought her soup.

'Where did you go?' Sugin leant her elbows on the table and put a hand under her chin, watching Cordelia intently as she ate.

Briefly Cordelia told her, hating being watched in such a way.

'There are many such places to go to in Sri Lanka. You must see them all. I will give you a list.'

For a moment Cordelia was surprised at the native girl's encouragement, but then realised that it would suit Sugin for her to go out sightseeing all the time because it would keep her away from Marcus, so she just gave a small polite smile and asked, 'Where did you learn to speak English so well? Have you been to England?'

Sugin shook her head proudly. 'It is not necessary to go to a foreign country to learn the language. I learn English at school—I am very good pupil. When I leave school I have job as guide in tea factory. Then I meet Charles Conran and I come here.'

'Charles Conran is the owner of the bungalow?' Cordelia hazarded.

Sugin nodded gracefully, as she did everything gracefully. 'Yes.' She looked at Cordelia through slanted, triumphant eyes. 'And now I am—with Marcus.'

'Oh, yes,' Cordelia agreed with soft venom. 'He told me you came with the bungalow—just like the rest of the furniture.'

She hadn't intended to be spiteful, after all it was none of her business, but the other girl's gloating malevolence had so put her back up that she hadn't been able to stop herself. For a moment the barb didn't sink in, but then Sugin bristled like one of the wild leopards in the game reserves. 'You should not stay here, English girl,' she spat out, 'Marcus does not want you here. You interfere with his work. That is why he gives you the car and tells Daya to keep you out all day. This is why he goes out at night. He does not wish to be here alone with you. You bore him, English girl. He wants you to go to a hotel.'

'He does—or you do?' Cordelia demanded, aware that it was open warfare between them.

'He does! He told me so—many times,' Sugin retorted angrily.

'I don't believe you. I . . .' Cordelia broke off as the houseboy brought her omelette and took her soup dish away. Somehow it seemed ridiculous to be having this kind of argument while she was trying to eat a meal, but to push her plate away would be some sort of victory for Sugin, so she forced herself to go on eating as calmly as she could.

'It is true. He does not want you here,' Sugin insisted. 'Your father can stay because he is a sick man. But Marcus wishes that you would go.'

'Really? I must ask him, then, mustn't I?'

If Cordelia had hoped to disconcert the other girl, she was disappointed. Sugin merely shrugged and said, 'He is too polite to tell you himself, but me he has told many times. He tells me many things. We have no secrets,' she added, emphasising the words.

Cordelia didn't have to have it spelled out for her; she was fully aware that Sugin must be his mistress. As calmly as she could, she finished her meal and wiped her lips. 'I expect you want to get home. Please don't let me keep you.'

Sugin smiled and shook her head. 'I am not going home tonight. Marcus has asked me to wait for him. So you might as well go to bed, English girl. He does not want you to wait for him again tonight.'

Only Marcus could have told Sugin that she had been up when he got home last night, and Cordelia flushed, wondering for the first time if there had been any truth in the other girl's words. Maybe he really didn't want her around, even though he had assured her that she and her father could stay as long as they needed to.

Seeing that she had scored a hit, Sugin went on, 'Why do you not go home, English girl? There is nothing for you in Sri Lanka.'

Annoyed, Cordelia stood up and retorted sharply, 'On the contrary, I have just as much right to be here as you have.'

'You? What do you mean?'

'I mean that I was born here too. I'm as Sri Lankan as you are.'

Which wasn't strictly true, but at least enabled her to walk out of the room leaving Sugin completely disconcerted.

Out in the hall, Cordelia found that her hands were trembling and she had to get a grip on herself before going across to tap softly on her father's door. He was asleep, so she spent some time sitting with the nurse and chatting quietly. It was the nurse's last night, she told Cordelia. The doctor had come this morning and said that his patient was well enough to leave and that in future a nurse would just come twice a day to help him to bathe and make sure he took his pills and was generally okay. Cordelia passed a pleasant hour with her, finding the woman intelligent and friendly. She also spoke English very well and said that all children were taught it in school as a second language as a matter of course, so it wasn't such a big thing as Sugin made out that she spoke English so fluently.

It was almost midnight when Cordelia finally turned out her light and lay awake in the darkness, listening, and it must have been nearly one before she heard Marcus come home. She strained her ears, trying to hear him talking to Sugin, but they must have been very quiet, because all she heard was the sound of his door shutting softly. Perhaps Sugin was already in his room, lying naked in his bed, waiting for him to come to her, Cordelia imagined restlessly, and was seized with such a violent fit of jealousy that she could cheerfully have got hold of Sugin and strangled her. But the next second she realised miserably that she was the intruder and that Marcus probably looked on her only as a silly young girl who had thrown herself at his head. Why else would he have told Sugin about last night? Had he even told the other girl that he'd kissed her? Cordelia wondered wretchedly. Had they laughed together about it? Another sound caught her attention and she realised that it was her father's nurse going into the kitchen to make herself a drink. She, too, had been awake late last night and could have heard her talking to Marcus. Maybe it was she who had mentioned it to Sugin. Slightly comforted, Cordelia tried to go to sleep, but her mind was filled with pictures of the two of them together and, even when fatigue overcame her, her dreams, too, were about them making love, so that she turned and murmured restlessly.

Next morning, she had to use make-up to

disguise the dark smudges of tiredness around her eyes. She wasn't looking forward to having to face the two of them, especially knowing that they had spent the night together; she could imagine the way Sugin would look at her with triumph in her dark eyes, the possessive way she would preside over the breakfast table, every movement calculated to emphasise the fact that she was not only Marcus's mistress but also virtually the mistress of his house and that Cordelia was only an unwanted interloper. And Marcus? Would his night of love show in his face, in his manner? Cordelia gripped her hairbrush and bit her lip hard. There was only one way, she decided, that she was going to get through today, and that was by acting as if he really was just her boss, by being brisk and impersonal and definitely not letting him see that she fancied him. Even so, she took as long as she could over getting ready, but she couldn't hang around in her room for ever, so eventually she went out on to the verandah.

To her surprise only Marcus was there, reading a letter from a small pile beside his plate. He stood up as she came out, his eyes running fleetingly over her.

'Good morning. How did you enjoy your sightseeing?'

Acting on her decision, she gave him a bright smile and answered, 'It was very interesting, thank you. Daya was a very good guide. We went to Dambulla and then on to Anuradhapura.'

'What did you think of them?'

Cordelia remembered all the interesting things she had stored up to tell him and resolutely pushed them aside. 'As I said, they were very interesting. Please don't let me stop you if you were reading your mail,' she added, and pointedly looked away to butter a piece of toast.

Marcus smiled lazily. 'Are you the type that prefers to start the morning in peace and quite? Who bury themselves in the morning paper to avoid having to make conversation over the coffee and toast?'

Shrugging her shoulders, Cordelia said, 'I don't know, really. I only ever eat breakfast when I'm on holiday; I don't bother with it when I'm at home.'

'Where's home?'

'I share a flat near Baker Street with three other girls.'

'And you work in an office, I think you said?'

'Yes.'

'What do you do in your leisure time?'

She shrugged again. 'We go to discos and the cinema quite a lot—and I'm taking a course of evening classes to learn book-keeping.'

'Very commendable,' Marcus commented on an amused note, then his voice changed as he said, 'No boy-friends?'

Cordelia choked a little over her coffee but managed to cover it with a cough. His eyes settled on her, but she didn't meet them. 'One or two.' She managed to say it offhandedly, then immediately put down her coffee cup and stood up. 'I expect you'd like me to start work now; I still have a lot to do before I catch up with you.'

Without waiting for him to answer, she walked along the verandah and went into the study, where she began to take the cover off the typewriter; the conversation had started to get too personal if she was to be able to stay brisk and businesslike. Marcus followed more slowly. He stood watching her for a moment, then remarked, 'You're very efficient this morning.'

'Am I? Well, there's a lot to do.'

'Is anything the matter?'

She allowed herself a brief glance in his direction. 'No, of course not. Why should there be?' She sat down and pulled his manuscript forward. 'What chapter did you get up to yesterday?'

'Chapter six.'

'Then you're still four ahead of me.'

His hand came down on to her shoulder and she had to stifle a gasp as his touch seemed to burn into her flesh. 'This isn't a race, you know,' he remarked gently.

Cordelia stiffened but didn't look up. Licking lips gone suddenly dry, she managed to say brightly, 'Oh, but I'm eager to read the rest of the book.'

His hand stayed where it was a moment longer, then he took it away and sat down at his desk. He didn't say anything further; after such a silly remark as hers there probably wasn't anything to say. Cordelia began to type and after a while had to take the sheet out of the machine when he wasn't looking because she'd made so many mistakes.

They worked on through the morning and when Marcus stopped for coffee she didn't take it with him but excused herself and went to see her father. When she came back there was a slightly sardonic curl to his mouth, but Marcus merely asked after the invalid.

'He seems much better, thank you. He's going to get up for a while this afternoon.'

'Good. I'm glad to hear he's making progress.'

Because then we'll be gone the sooner? Cordelia wondered. So that he can be alone with Sugin again. There had been no sign of the other girl this morning, but Cordelia was fully expecting her to put in an appearance at lunchtime and was agreeably surprised when she saw that the table had been set for only two. Perhaps Sugin was still recovering from last night, she thought, with a flash of emotion which was as much jealousy as bitchiness. Not that Marcus's face showed any sign of tiredness or dissipation; she studied him covertly as she ate, listening as he talked about the chapter of the book he was working on. Her eyes ran over his aggressively handsome features, the wide breadth of his shoulders, and lingered on the play of the muscles in his bare, tanned arms. She wondered what he would be like in bed.

Almost as if she had said the words aloud, Marcus suddenly fell silent and looked at her. Their eyes met and held and Cordelia felt her face suffuse with colour, so that if there had been any doubt in his mind before about what she was thinking, there was certainly none now. Hastily she looked away and began to eat feverishly. The silence seemed to go on for ever, but at last he began to talk again, picking up from where he had left off. But the amusement in his voice was quite clear. Damn you, Cordelia swore inwardly. Stop laughing at me, damn you! She didn't dare look at him in case she blushed again, and luckily he didn't ask her any questions, just went on talking easily until they had finished and went back to work again.

Somehow she managed to pull herself together and get through the rest of the afternoon and dinner, but gave a sigh of relief when Marcus afterwards went in to sit with her father and she was able to go to her room with a book and not see him any more that night. He had offered her the car again for another sightseeing trip the next day, but the driver had reported that there was a part that needed replacing and had taken it to a garage which promised it back in two days. 'But knowing Sri Lankan garages it could be anything up to two weeks,' Marcus had remarked wryly.

The next two days were better; Cordelia was more in control of herself, had managed to get things back in proportion and was able to keep the hours they were alone together on an impersonal but friendly level, if such a thing were possible. Marcus went along with it, although once or twice she found him watching her with that sardonically amused look on his lean features. After dinner they both went in to sit with James Allingham and had a game of gin rummy with him. Cordelia was amazed at the way her father's personality changed when he was with Marcus; he talked far more than he ever did with her, especially when Marcus drew him out on his years managing the tea plantation, and he even laughed a few times at his own experiences. Perhaps it was that he preferred men's company, Cordelia surmised, and excused herself quite early on the plea of being tired, hoping that he would expand even more without her presence to restrict him.

On the third day they had breakfasted and Cordelia had started work when Marcus stepped briskly into the room, swung her chair round and pulled her to her feet. 'No work today! Contrary to my pessimistic view the car's been repaired as promised and you're taking the day off.'

'Oh, but I was in the middle of . . .' She went to

sit down again, but he kept hold of her wrists and wouldn't let her.

'Oh, no, you don't. You heard me—we're going sightseeing.'

Cordelia stared at him. 'We?'

'Yes. It's Daya's day off, so I'm afraid you'll have to put up with me as your guide.' His eyes glinted down into hers. 'Do you mind?'

Her heart began to beat much too fast and her throat was so dry that she stammered as she said, 'N-no, of course not.'

'Good.' He smiled down at her, his mouth slightly more curved one side than the other, which stupidly made her heart give a crazy lurch. 'You have twenty minutes to get ready.' Then he was gone and she heard him giving orders to someone in the kitchen. For a few minutes she stood still, too overwhelmed by surprise, excitement and anticipation to do anything but stare after him. All her good resolutions about being brisk and impersonal had evaporated into thin air, dissolved into nothing before the word we—'*We* are going sightseeing.' Sugin might not have existed, the affair between them be only a figment of her imagination. Nothing mattered except that she and Marcus were going to spend the day together.

Poking his head back into the room, Marcus saw her still standing there and said with mock severity, 'Fifteen minutes!'

Cordelia suddenly came to life. Laughing happily, she covered the typewriter and ran to change into a pale blue sundress that matched her eyes and a pair of wedge-heeled, comfortable sandals. Grabbing up her bag and the other things she needed for the day, she ran out to the front of

the house, a faint flush on her cheeks and all the
excitement she felt showing in her eyes.

Marcus looked up from stowing a hamper in the
boot of the car, an arrested expression on his face.
'You look like a child who's been promised a
treat.'

Cordelia smiled at him fully for the first time in
three days. 'I feel like one,' she told him happily.
'Where are we going?'

'Get in and I'll show you on the map.'

He had a big map of the island and as he sat
next to her he handed it to her and helped her to
spread it out on her lap. Leaning across, he
pointed out the route he intended to take. 'You
covered most of the road when you went with
Daya, but today we're turning off to Sigiriya—
here.' He pointed with a long finger. 'There's
plenty of time, we don't have to rush, so if you see
anywhere on the way that you want to stop and
look at, just give a yell.'

'Yes, all right.' Her eyes weren't on the map but
on his profile, following the hard outline of his
face, her nostrils full of his freshly applied
aftershave. It had a musky tang to it that made her
want to get closer.

The day was hot and sunny and, as usual, the
roads were full of people, but Marcus took his
time and didn't drive on his brakes as Daya did, so
that she didn't have to keep grabbing at the
dashboard to steady herself. They stopped at a
level-crossing to wait for the train to go by and
where there was a big open market full of people,
most of the sellers with their wares carried in on
their backs and displayed in baskets or spread out
on the ground on pieces of sacking. There were
spiky pineapples and the rich purple sheen of

mangosteens and the brilliant scarlet of chilli peppers that had been dried in the sun. But above everything was the noise of the people as they haggled loudly over their purchases, carrying umbrellas to guard them from the sun and the occasional monsoon shower. The train came along, old and dirty and packed with people, and the gates swung open. For a while the road ran alongside the single railway track, which was almost as busy as the road, with the people walking along it using it as a short cut to the next village, and with much less chance of being knocked down and killed, Cordelia guessed wryly as she watched them.

They stopped for her to take photos of an ornate painted Hindu temple covered with carvings of figures that each seemed to have an unbelievable number of arms and heads, and again at a batik factory where they were shown the waxing and dyeing processes and where Cordelia tried on and bought several dresses that had the most beautiful designs and were incredibly cheap. She had thought that Marcus might get impatient with her for spending so long in the batik shop, but he wasn't in the least; he even picked out a couple of dresses for her to try on which he said he thought would suit her. Needless to say, she bought them both.

Back in the car, Marcus drove northwards again, through an open plain with occasional villages scattered alongside the main road, with beyond them a few cultivated fields before the scrublike-looking trees that Marcus told her was the start of what the Sri Lankans called the jungle area, although it was so very open and sparse that Cordelia would never have described it as that

herself. Every now and again there were huge
outcrops of rock sticking up out of the plain like
giant-size versions of the anthills that she saw at
the sides of the road. Pointing ahead, Marcus said,
'See that huge circular rock with the flat top up
ahead? That's Sigiriya where we're heading. They
call it the Lion Rock.'

The rock was massive, more like a small
mountain; it rose red-gold from its surrounding
belt of trees to stand sentinel against the blue of
the cloudless sky. When they neared it they had to
stop and buy tickets before they could go any
farther, but Marcus refused the services of a guide
and drove on to park the car under the shade of
some trees.

'I thought we might have a stroll round the
ruins of the summer palace first, then have lunch
and a rest before we attempt the climb up the
rock. Okay by you?'

'Mm, fine.' Cordelia followed him out of the
car, perfectly happy to go anywhere he cared to
suggest. They wandered slowly round the ruins
under the hot sun, Marcus pointing out where the
different parts of the palace had stood. The day
was very still and sultry and the only other people
exploring the ruins were a long way off, near the
foot of the Lion Rock. Cordelia had a feeling of
timelessness, when she stood still and half closed
her eyes she could almost see the ancient people
who had inhabited these vast ruins.

'What are you thinking?' Marcus's soft question
brought her out of her reverie.

'Oh, nothing really.'

'Nothing?' His eyebrows lifted in disbelief.

'Well,' she gave a half embarrassed laugh, 'only
that if you closed your eyes you could imagine

what it must have been like—the people who lived here then, the way it must have been.'

She expected him to laugh at her, or worse, see that sardonically mocking look in his face, but to her surprise he nodded and said quickly, 'That's right, there's an aura about the place. You can see the king sitting in his throne room, his warriors about him and dozens of the most beautiful women dancing for him and attending to his needs.'

Cordelia smiled. 'I hadn't imagined the bit about the beautiful women.'

Marcus laughed and slipped a casual arm round her waist. 'But at least you have an imagination. The last people I brought here just said, "Oh, yes" politely to everything I pointed out and couldn't wait to get to the nearest hotel with a bar.'

'Who was that?' Cordelia asked, warm from his praise and his touch.

'Oh, just some people who came over for a short visit from England.' He paused and looked away from her, was silent for a few minutes, then said almost to himself, 'I suppose that's really all they are—just a lot of old stones. Unless you have the imagination to clothe them in history.' He turned to Cordelia and let his eyes run over her tall, youthfully slim figure. 'As you have,' he said softly.

Cordelia gazed at him, sensing that there was something deeper behind his words, waiting, longing for him to go on, to confide in her, but then his eyebrows flickered at the imperative honking of a tourist coach on the nearby road and the moment was lost. He grinned at her and caught hold of her hand. 'But I bet right now you'd much rather have a glass of chilled white wine.'

'Did you say *chilled*? Just lead me to it!' Cordelia agreed fervently, and let him run her along to the car, protesting laughingly, 'You didn't mean it, did you? You haven't really got cold wine?'

But he had. He opened up the picnic hamper and revealed two bottles of wine in a special container to keep them cool.

'You,' Cordelia informed him in awestruck tones, 'are definitely the man I would most like to be marooned on a desert island with. You get my vote every time!' He passed her a glass and she drank it slowly, savouring every drop, letting it linger in her dry throat and passing her tongue over her lips. 'Oh, that was good,' she sighed reverently. 'The best drink I've ever tasted. Nectar!'

'The drink of the gods.' He took the empty glass from her and said softly, 'Your lips are wet with wine. They make me want to taste them.'

'D-do they?' Cordelia breathed, her heart standing still.

'Yes.' And he bent forward and put his mouth on hers, softly, gently, letting his lips explore its full softness, then he drew back and looked down into her rapt face. Slowly Cordelia opened her eyes; only their mouths had touched and yet she felt as if he had touched and explored her whole body, every nerve end was on fire and her heart now was racing crazily. Marcus refilled her glass and gave it to her, then filled his own and raised it. 'To all the ancient pagan gods,' he toasted, his eyes smiling lazily into hers.

'Especially to Bacchus,' Cordelia added, trying to keep her tone as light as his.

'Most definitely,' Marcus agreed with a grin. 'Now what have they given us to eat?'

So they sat in the shade of the trees in that ancient place and ate and drank, taking their time, talking and laughing often. Somehow Cordelia found herself telling him all about her life in Sri Lanka, and then back in England alone with her mother and aunt, not realising that she was betraying a great deal more to him than just her words conveyed. Then she asked him about himself, but he again evaded the question. 'Maybe one day I'll write my autobiography and you'll be able to read it all,' he told her, lying back in the grass, his head pillowed on his arms.

'Afraid I'll reveal all the sordid details of your life to the gutter press, huh?' Cordelia teased him. She stretched out alongside him, lying on her stomach, her head propped up on her elbows.

His lips curled into that slightly crooked grin. 'Watch it, woman, or I'll put you in my autobiography!'

'Really?' Cordelia was intrigued. 'What would you say?'

He had closed his eyes, but now he opened them a little and looked at her lazily. 'Well, that would depend.'

'On what?'

'On whether or not you're going to kiss me, of course.'

Cordelia had been toying idly with the gold necklace she wore, but now her fingers grew still as she stared down at him, not sure whether he was teasing or serious. But he merely gave a small grin and closed his eyes again, which was no help at all. She looked down at his face for several minutes, noticing how the lock of dark hair that had fallen

forward on his forehead softened the hardness of
his features. And there was a small cleft in his chin
which made her want to run her finger along it.
Slowly she edged a little nearer. His breathing was
quite regular and she thought he had fallen
asleep, so she was quite safe. Even in repose there
was a harsh look to his mouth and she saw now
that they were lines of bitterness that had given it
that slightly sardonic curve. Cordelia found that
she very much wanted to kiss those lines away, to
make them disappear for ever. She leaned over
him, confident that he was asleep, her eyes
studying his face. Slowly she lowered her head and
just touched his lips with her own, the pressure no
greater than the flutter of a butterfly's wing. But
even so, Marcus had felt it, and when she went to
lift her head away he put a hand behind her neck
so that she couldn't move. His eyes opened and
looked into hers. 'You can do better than that,' he
told her softly.

'Yes.' The word was no more than a sigh.

'Then show me.'

She lowered her head again, her hair falling
forward and forming a golden curtain around their
heads. Her lips found his and touched them gently
in small kisses, each of which was a caress,
demanding nothing but giving freely of their
warmth and softness. He lay there, letting her take
his mouth, but when Cordelia parted his lips with
her tongue she felt a quiver run through him, his
hand tightened on her neck and he began to kiss
her passionately in return. Pulled off balance, she
fell against him and immediately Marcus's arm
went round her, holding her close, half lying on
top of him. Cordelia's arms went round his neck
as she responded, overwhelmed by his sudden

passion, lost to everything around her. But then Marcus abruptly pushed her away and sat up and she became aware of voices nearby. A party of Sri Lankan pilgrims headed by two Buddhist monks in their saffron robes were walking through the ruins towards them. Cordelia gave them one glance, then turned back to stare at Marcus, her hair dishevelled, chest heaving, her eyes still bemused with passion.

Marcus's eyes settled on her face for a long moment, then he quickly got to his feet and pulled her up beside him. 'Let's go up to the fortress. It should be a little cooler now.'

Cordelia put up a hand to push the hair away from her face, a hand that wasn't quite steady. 'Yes. All right.' She helped him to pack up the picnic things and stow them in the car, acting mechanically, her mind still lost in the clouds.

Marcus drove to the car park at the foot of the Lion Rock and they walked up the path between the little souvenir stalls selling ebony Buddhas, brightly-coloured balsa-wood masks and beaten brassware. They paused near a huge overhanging rock while Marcus told her how the Buddhists had taken over the place after the king who built the fortress had been defeated in battle. But she wasn't really listening; she was aware only of sensations: of the sun hot on her back, the murmur of his voice, of a lizard that crouched on a stone, watching her, most of all of Marcus's closeness, his shoulder almost touching hers; she only had to move a few inches and she would be able to lean against him, feel the length of his body against her own. She quivered, the desire so great that it became physical. Marcus's voice trailed off, Cordelia turned her head to look at him and their eyes met and held. She couldn't read his face, but hers must have been plain enough, because he smiled a little, then lifted a finger and lightly touched her lips. 'Later,' he murmured.

They moved on up through the trees and began to climb up the steps, Marcus acting as guide. Then the way became steep and narrow, with only a handrail between the path and a sheer drop down the side of the rock. And to reach the cave paintings they had to go up a spiral metal staircase attached to the bare rock face. The frescoes were rather disappointing, just a few paintings were left where once there had been hundreds. They were all of native girls, painted from the waist up in gentle orange, pink and green colours. They were adorned with jewelled headdresses, necklaces and countless bracelets, and they all had beautifully rounded, and quite bare, breasts.

'They call them the Cloud Maidens,' Marcus told her. 'Because we're so high up, I suppose.'

'I don't see any paintings of men,' Cordelia noted drily.

'Of course not. These ancient kings knew how to get their priorities right.'

'You mean they date from the Early Chauvinist Age?'

Marcus's laugh echoed round the shallow cave in which they stood. Putting a hand on her arm, he said, 'You know, you make me realise what I've been missing while I've been here.'

Cordelia didn't ask him to explain. To see him smile, to feel his hand on her arm, was enough. She felt as high as the Cloud Maidens, her heart soaring dizzily. They went back down the spiral stairs and Marcus helped her because she wasn't that good on heights. She was terribly aware of him, every time he touched her, even of his closeness; it was as if there was some sort of electric current running between them that set off sparks every time they touched.

Walking round to the other side of the rock they came to a place where once the massive head of a lion crouching on its paws had stood guard over the entrance to the upper fortress on top of the rock. Now only the paws remained on either side of some steps that had once gone through the archway of the lion's mouth. Above the steps there was an iron ladder with a handrail attached to the rock face.

'Do you want to try it?' Marcus asked her.

Cordelia hesitated as she looked up the sheer climb. 'Have you ever been up there?' she asked doubtfully.

'Yes. But don't try it if you'd rather not.'

She gulped. 'I'll try.'

Going up the first part wasn't too bad, but then there was a tricky place which was just narrow, worn footsteps in the granite with only a low handrail to hold on to, but Marcus put a firm hand on her arm and she was up before she knew it. On the very top of the rock there were more ruins, and they wandered round for an hour or so, exploring. Then they had to get down. Cordelia found this a hundred times worse because you could see the drop below, and there was one really nasty moment when some people coming up wanted to pass. Almost she panicked, but Marcus put his arm round, her, talking to her matter-of-factly, and somehow the other people were past and they were safely down to the lion's paws again.

Marcus sat her down and went over to a drinks

stall under a tree which described itself as a 'Cool Spot' and brought her back a Coke. 'Here. 'Fraid it's not very cold, though.'

'Oh, *thanks*!' Cordelia drank thirstily and put up a hand to wipe the perspiration from her brow.

'You were scared stiff during that climb, weren't you?' Marcus observed accusingly. And when she nodded, he went on, 'So why did you do it?'

She shrugged. 'Because I wanted to get to the top. I didn't want to be beaten.'

He looked amused. 'And do you always go after what you want so determinedly? Even though you're afraid?'

Cordelia set down the empty bottle of Coke and said lightly, 'I suppose that depends on how badly I want something. Aren't you willing to take a risk if you want something badly enough?'

His eyes rested on her face, flushed from the climb, and he nodded. 'Yes. And I always get what I want.'

'Always?'

'Yes. Always,' he answered firmly.

'How spoilt you must be, then,' Cordelia observed, wrinkling her nose at him.

He laughed, 'Hopelessly!' and reached out to take her hand and lead her back down the hill.

They didn't hurry on the drive back to the bungalow. Nor did they hurry over dinner afterwards, but both of them were aware of the physical tension and of the word 'later' that lay between them. They chatted easily over the meal, like people who had known each other a long time. Cordelia had pushed Sugin's shadow far into the background; she hadn't seen the other girl for three days and she certainly wasn't going to ask where she was. Occasionally, accidentally—or almost accidentally—their hands would touch, and Cordelia would almost gasp aloud. She had never before known such desire, such intense physical need.

When they had finished, Marcus stood up. 'Let's go for a stroll round the garden, shall we?' He took her hand and together they walked across the verandah and down into the warm scented garden.

They walked on until they had outdistanced the light thrown by the lamps in the house and there was only the moonlight to guide them. Marcus paused near the frangipani tree, its white flowers luminous in the soft rays of the moonlight. Leaning against the trunk of the tree, he pulled her gently towards him. 'Cordelia,' he breathed, his arms going round her, 'how lovely you look! So fair, so very fair.' He kissed her gently at first, then lifted his head to watch the moonlight play on the golden silk of her hair as he let it run through his fingers.

Cordelia stood it for as long as she could, but the touch of his fingers drove her mad. She dug her fingers into his shoulders and said his name on a little moan of need. 'Marcus.' He gave a low chuckle and put his hands down low on her hips, pulling her against him so that she gasped at his hardness. Then his mouth was on hers, fierce and demanding, and she surrendered happily to his blazing passion.

He kissed her again and again, his lips finding her eyes, her throat, setting her blood on fire. His hands went to her shoulders and pulled down the thin straps of her dress so that it hung from the belt at her waist. He tried to push her away a little so that he could look at her, but Cordelia clung to him, wanting to stay close. Firmly, then, he took hold of her hands so that she had to reluctantly move a step backwards. His eyes dwelt on the curve of her breasts, shadowed by the moonlight. 'You're beautiful,' he breathed thickly. 'Perfect. Like the Cloud Maidens.' Lifting his hands, he cupped her breasts, caressed them so that they hardened as she gasped with delight.

'But I'm real. I'm alive,' she managed to say, and impatiently pulled his head down to kiss him. She didn't give a damn about the Cloud Maidens, all she wanted was for Marcus to go on kissing and caressing her and never, ever stop. His lips took hers hungrily and then moved down to her breasts, making her give low, animal moans of pleasure. 'Oh, my darling,' she gasped. 'My love, my love!' His breath seemed to scorch her skin and she pressed herself against him, his hardness driving her crazy with longing. Putting his arms round her, Marcus held her still, her head against the hammering beat of his heart. When she tried to move he wouldn't let her, made her stay still for several long minutes, until his heart had retained a normal beat and her pulses had stopped racing quite so much.

Lifting her head at last, Cordelia looked at him questioningly. 'Marcus?'

He didn't answer, merely kissed her lightly on the forehead, slipped her dress back on her shoulders and then put his arm round her waist and led her back through the garden towards the house. Cordelia went with him willingly, her heart large and unruly in its beat. Her eyes were brilliant in her flushed face, as if lit from within, and she could think of nothing but the present, the here and now of being with Marcus, of feeling his arm around her, of going wherever he wanted to take her. And she fully expected that he was taking her to his bed. Short of him throwing her down on the ground, they had gone about as far as they could go, out there in the garden. It was natural now that he should take her back to the house, back to the nearest bed. The thought filled her with shy, excited anticipation, but no shame. The searing emotion and need he had aroused in her had been too intense for that. She wanted him as much as he seemed to want her. Never before had she experienced such a need for fulfilment, the urgent craving to be taken by a man—no, not any man, just this man, no one else.

She stumbled a little as they went up the steps to the verandah and Marcus's arm tightened round her waist. Cordelia laughed rather raggedly. 'My legs seem to have turned to jelly!'

He paused and looked down at her, a small frown between his dark brows. 'Cordelia, I . . .' His voice held a slightly troubled note, but he was unable to go on because Cordelia put her arms round his neck and leant her weight against him.

'I'm afraid you'll have to hold me up; my legs have no strength at all. You see what you've done to me?' she added with another excited laugh. Her grip tightened and her voice grew husky with emotion. 'Oh, Marcus. Darling, dearest Marcus! Today has been such a wonderful day. I shall never forget it, not as long as I live.'

Reaching up, he took her hands from round his neck, held them as his face, dark in the shadowed night, looked down into hers. Then he gently bent to kiss her lips, almost, Cordelia thought strangely, as if with regret or sadness.

'You must be tired. You'd better go in.'

'Yes.' She went ahead of him for a few steps, then turned. 'Aren't you—aren't you coming in too?' It was as close as she could get to an invitation, the nearest thing to saying, 'I want you to take me to your bed. I want you to love me.'

He seemed to murmur something under his breath, something she didn't catch, and she hadn't the courage to ask him again. He stood, a tall, dark shadow against the darker shadow of the night, unmoving, waiting for her to go. Quickly Cordelia turned on her heel and almost ran to her room. She prepared for bed eagerly, putting on her newest nightdress, brushing her hair until it shone, her hands trembling, her body aching for him. Turning off the lights, she left only a small lamp burning and opened her door on to the verandah in case he came that way.

But he didn't come. She waited until the house had been quiet for a long time before she turned off the light and got into bed. But even though the physical disappointment was intense, she wasn't unhappy. It had all happened so fast, like a carousel whirling round out of control, perhaps it was better this way. After all, they had plenty of time, all the time in the world. There was tomorrow, and all the tomorrows after that when they would be together. The future stretched into infinity and Cordelia smiled as she drifted into sleep.

CHAPTER FIVE

As usual, Marcus was up before her, even though Cordelia got up as soon as she awoke. He was sitting at the breakfast table, reading the local paper, and looked up when he heard her quick footsteps. She gave him a wonderful smile, her heart on her face, her blue eyes alight with happiness. 'Good morning.'

'Good morning.' He put down the paper and poured her a cup of coffee. 'You look very well this morning.'

'I feel well. I feel terrific.' She smiled again, her eyes warm as they dwelt almost hungrily on his face. 'You know I do.'

A brief frown covered his forehead, but then the houseboy came to bring her breakfast, and when she looked again the frown had gone. Marcus stood up. 'Would you excuse me? I have some telephoning to do.'

He was gone some time; she'd finished eating and had looked at the paper by the time he came back. She got quickly to her feet. 'I'm ready to start work.'

'Don't you think you ought to go and see how your father is? You hardly saw him yesterday,' Marcus reminded her.

'Oh, yes, of course. I'll be right back.' She laughed up at him and touched his hand. 'Don't start without me.'

James Allingham was seated in a chair by the window, playing a game of patience. For once he seemed quite pleased to see her and even asked her about her trip to Sigiriya, telling her about a visit he had made to it about thirty years ago. Cordelia listened as patiently as she could, while all the time longing to get back to Marcus. At length she cut her father short, explaining that their host was waiting for her to do some typing for him. It was near enough the truth. She hurried from his room without regret; her father had dismissed her enough in the past week for her to feel it.

Marcus was working at his desk, his back towards her as she slipped into the room. Quietly, an impish smile on her lips, Cordelia crept up behind him and put her hands over his eyes. 'Guess who?' she breathed.

He half turned round and lifted up an arm to pull her hands away, but Cordelia slipped on to his lap, leaving one arm round his neck and with the other gently tracing the outline of his lips with her finger. Then she kissed him, lingeringly, reliving all over again the thrill of his mouth on hers.

He didn't respond, but he didn't draw away either; just let her go on kissing him, and when she looked at him with questioning doubt, only gave that crooked grin and said, 'Delightful as that sort of thing can be, young lady, it isn't helping to get this book finished.'

Slowly she stood up. 'You—you mean there's a time and a place for everything?'

'Something like that.' He swung back to his desk and bent his head to his work again.

Cordelia went to her own desk and stared at his bent head. She felt like a teenager who'd tried to do something grown up, only to be told that she was still a child. Didn't he feel the same as she did?

She wanted to be near him, to touch, to see him, and she didn't care where or what time of the day it was. To confirm all that yesterday, and especially last night, had meant to her. Unless it had all meant nothing to him. But surely not. He couldn't have kissed her like that without it meaning anything at all. She had to know, had to ask him. 'Marcus . . .' she began.

But he cut in at once, his voice brusque. 'I've put the next chapter to be typed just by the typewriter.'

After a long pause, Cordelia picked up a piece of paper and put it in the machine, then began to type.

Just before lunch, there was the sound of a car outside and Marcus went out to see who it was. He came back with another man, younger than himself, perhaps in his late twenties; a tall man with brown hair bleached by the sun and a darkly tanned body revealed by his short-sleeved shirt that was open to the waist of his tight-fitting jeans.

'Cordelia, this is Steve Randall. He's working up on the dam they're building up in the hills. You remember, I told you about it.'

'Yes, of course. How do you do, Mr Randall?'

The young man laughed. 'You're very formal! We all call one another by our Christian names out here.'

'Let's go outside and have a drink before lunch.' Marcus led the way out on to the verandah and they sat at the white-painted table while they waited for the houseboy to bring the drinks.

'Marcus told us all about the accident you had,' Steve told her. 'How is your father now?'

'Recovering quite well, thank you.' Cordelia

wished the man wasn't there, wished Marcus didn't seem so pleased to see him.

'Must have given you quite a fright. Has the doc said when he'll be well enough to be moved?'

'No, not yet. He had a heart attack, you see; that's what made him crash,' she felt impelled to add. Her eyes kept going to Marcus, but he was looking down at his drink.

Steve started asking her about her life in England and it became apparent that he expected to stay to lunch. From his talk with Marcus she gathered that he was one of his friends from the Expatriates Club and that on the evenings Marcus went there they mostly played poker or some other card game. But he didn't talk to Marcus too much, most of his attention he gave to Cordelia, telling her about the dam he was working on, with some really funny anecdotes about the differences and misunderstandings that often arose with the native labour force. 'Sometimes, when I shout at them for being too slow or for doing something stupidly dangerous,' he told her, 'they refuse to do any more work. Then we send for *my* boss, who's another Englishman, and he pretends to shout at me for shouting at *them*, and that makes them happy again and they all go back to work.'

Marcus grinned and encouraged him to go on. He took little part in the conversation himself, which was unusual; not that Cordelia said very much, she merely smiled and put in suitable remarks and questions at appropriate moments. Every other minute her eyes would go back to Marcus, seeing some sign, some acceptance from him of their closer involvement. A look that was for her alone, a smile, a touch of hands, even a wink would have lifted her back into the clouds.

Once their eyes did meet and he did smile, but it was a casual, impersonal smile, meaning nothing. If he had deliberately looked away, avoided her eyes, Cordelia would have known that something was wrong and she could have tried to do something about it, but against apparent indifference she was completely helpless.

When they had finished lunch and were lingering over coffee, Steve said to Marcus, 'Where's Sugin? I haven't seen her around today.'

'Her sister is ill. She's gone to look after her for a few days.'

'Her sister doesn't live over at her mother's place, then?'

'No, her sister's married and lives over in Nuwara Eliya,' Marcus answered dismissively.

So Steve knew all about Sugin, and presumably that she was Marcus's mistress, Cordelia realised unhappily. Since last night she hadn't given much thought to Sugin, but now she began to wonder if it was because of her that Marcus seemed so offhand. Had he just been amusing himself with her while Sugin wasn't around? And had he now decided that he preferred the other girl? He ought to, she supposed, trying to be realistic; after all, theirs had been a much longer relationship.

'What places have you visited in Sri Lanka, Cordelia?' Steve's voice interrupted her thoughts and she was forced to concentrate on answering him.

'Have you been to Colombo yet?' She admitted that she hadn't and he immediately said, 'Hey, why don't we go over there this afternoon? We could see the sights and then we could go over to the Intercontinental to swim and then have dinner there.' He looked at them both eagerly. 'How about it? If we left now we could be in Colombo in a couple of hours. You'd like to go, wouldn't you, Cordelia?'

Cordelia didn't, not in the least. 'I've been helping Marcus with his work,' she temporised. 'I know he wants to get on.'

'Nonsense, you're on holiday,' said Marcus. 'And you ought to see Colombo.' He paused for a moment, then glanced at Steve. 'I think it's a great idea. Let's all go.' He got to his feet and looked down at her. 'Cordelia?'

'Yes, okay. Give me ten minutes to get ready.'

She hurried to her room, grateful that Marcus hadn't tried to push her off on to Steve. For a few moments back there she had been certain that that was what he intended to do, that he would make work his excuse to stay behind. But if he had, she wouldn't have gone, she would have insisted on staying to help him. She started to wonder if Steve had been invited over just to take her off Marcus's hands, and the thought chilled her through to her bones.

They went in Marcus's car, it having been chosen as more comfortable for her than the Land Rover Steve had borrowed from the dam workings, which meant that Marcus drove with Cordelia in the front seat beside him and Steve leaning forward in the space between the seats, his arms reaching along their backs. Cordelia hadn't travelled along the road before, so there were plenty of places of interest for Steve to point out to her, including a mountain known as Adam's Peak.

'You'll have to go and see that, Cordelia,' Steve enthused. 'You have to get to the top before dawn because then a bank of clouds blows into the

valley below and for a brief moment the sun
catches it and somehow casts the shadow of the
mountain on to the mass of clouds. It's almost like
a—what do you call those things they have in the
desert?'

'A mirage,' Marcus supplied.

'Yeah, that's right.'

'Or an illusion,' Cordelia added drily.

Marcus shot her a quick look under hooded
lids, but Steve innocently assured her, 'No, you
can see it all right, it's really there.'

'Have you seen it?' She made an effort to keep
the conversation going—after all, it wasn't
Steve's fault that there was this tension building up
in her.

'No, but some of the other men have. They say
it's well worth making the effort to go there. Why
don't we go and see it together?' he suggested.

Cordelia didn't know whether the 'we' included
Marcus, but she said lightly anyway, 'Why not?'
having no intention of going with him. If she had
been alone with Marcus, then yes, oh yes; it would
have been a magical experience, but she didn't
want to go with anyone else, even somebody as
well-intentioned as Steve.

When they reached Colombo, they stopped for a
drink and then Marcus drove her round the city so
that she could see the reproduction of the giant
standing statue of Buddha at Aukana, the
imposing monument to Mrs Bandaranaike given
to Sri Lanka by the People's Republic of China,
and the television station given to the people of Sri
Lanka by Japan.

'So that they'd buy Japanese television sets,'
Marcus remarked sourly. They drove through
streets even more crowded and chaotic than any

she'd seen before and honked imperatively at little
three-wheeled, two-seater electric taxis with
canopies like a pram that you could put up when it
rained. They passed the rose-pink buildings,
known as the Fort, that covered a whole block and
housed Colombo's principal shopping centre, then
Marcus drove into the forecourt of the nearby
Intercontinental Hotel.

They were all glad to get there and with one
accord headed for the bar.

'This country always makes me feel so dry,'
Cordelia commented. 'I'm always thirsty.'

'Me too,' Steve agreed, looking with loving
anticipation at the huge glass of cold beer the
bartender was pouring for him. He sat on a bar
stool next to her and Marcus moved to her other
side. For a while they just sat and drank in
grateful silence, then Cordelia's bare arm happened
to touch Marcus's elbow and she began to tremble
as if she'd been scorched. She couldn't look at
him, was afraid to, in case he saw the desolation in
her face, so she determinedly turned to Steve and
began to talk to him animatedly, although for the
life of her afterwards she couldn't think what it
was about.

When they had finished their drinks, they
changed into swimsuits and walked down to the
nearby beach to bathe. There was some tide and
rolling waves, but they weren't very rough and it
was comfortable to swim there. Cordelia wasn't
that good and stayed within her depth, but the two
men raced each other far out. She watched them
and had visions of sharks and cramp, and
breathed a sigh of relief when they came back
safely. They all began to play around in the surf,
chasing one another and diving down under the

waves. Once Steve went under the water and caught hold of her legs, trying to duck her, but Cordelia kicked free and knifed away, but bumped into Marcus who was behind her. His arms went round her to prevent her from going under and for a moment she lay against him, their bodies touching. He looked beautiful stripped nearly naked as he was, not as obviously beefy as Steve perhaps, but tanned and muscular and athletic, with strong legs and a slim waist beneath the breadth of his shoulders. And there was a mat of dark hairs on his chest where the water clung in glistening drops. Cordelia wanted to lick away each drop, to taste the warm saltiness of his skin. She must have made some sound, because his hands tightened, hurting her, and for a moment his face was open and she thought she read desire in his eyes, but almost instantly it was gone and he laughed and said, 'Let's get him, shall we?' and she found herself being pulled into chasing Steve and trying to duck him.

After about an hour they went back to the hotel and sat around in loungers, sunbathing until the sun went down, drinking, smoking and talking desultorily. The two men seemed to know each other quite well, they were at ease with one another and had 'in' jokes that meant nothing to Cordelia. It seemed that they had arrived in Sri Lanka more or less at the same time, Steve having signed a two-year contract with the dam construction company. Intellectually they were probably very different; Steve was a far more practical type than Marcus, a man of action who was used to giving orders and being responsible for the people under him. He was gregarious, an extrovert, whereas Marcus was more of a loner, happy to share the company of others but needing often to be quite private and alone, and never finding his own company boring. He was well read too, understandably, which Steve wasn't, and Marcus was capable of taking a conversation to far greater depths than the younger man could.

The hotel provided changing rooms for visitors, so Cordelia was able to shower the sea salt and sun oil from her skin and change into a dress she had brought with her. It was pale yellow with a halter neck, no back at all and a full, pleated skirt. It looked good against her tan. Her hair, too, when she had dried it with the blow-dryer provided by the hotel, gleamed a lighter gold from the sun. She looked golden all over; her dress, the honey gold of her skin, her hair; she even had gold sandals for her feet.

The men were waiting for her when she came out. As she walked down the corridor they both looked her over, the way a man does look at a woman, speculatively, his eyes going down over her body. Steve's gaze became frankly admiring, but she couldn't read Marcus's face, he had the ability to completely hide his feelings. She walked between them into the dining-room and every head in the place seemed to turn in their direction as they were shown to their table. The glances of the women were frankly envious as they saw her with the two tall, good-looking men, and those of the men weren't exactly unappreciative either, which gave Cordelia a much-needed boost to her ego.

Their table became a centre of laughter and gaiety; Cordelia putting herself out to sparkle and amuse. Steve lapped it up, obviously enjoying himself hugely, and Marcus, too, joined in and

appeared to be getting a kick out of the evening.
Whether he was acting a part, Cordelia wasn't at
all sure, but once or twice she caught him looking
at her with an abstracted frown in his eyes. And
she was definitely putting on an act, giving
everything to it like a star hoping to win an Oscar.
She drank quite a bit, too, but didn't even feel
lightheaded.

After dinner they went into the night club
attached to the hotel and drank cocktails based on
arrack, a locally made spirit very similar to
whisky. A local group played their version of the
European hit numbers, much too loud, of course,
but then all discos everywhere were much too
loud, after a while you gave up trying to talk and
just let the music wash over you, the beat get into
your bones. There were other European women
there, nearly all married and with their men, just
here and there an odd girl watched over anxiously
by her parents or two girls together who were soon
dancing with some European men who were also
on their own. Cordelia peered round in the
comparative gloom looking for the Sri Lankan
women, but the only ones who looked dark
enough to be natives wore European dress and
stayed close to the sides of the men they were with.
There were plenty of young native men there,
though; all impossibly slim and neatly dressed, and
obviously on the prowl, looking for European girls
to dance with. One came up and asked Cordelia
almost before she'd walked into the place, but she
didn't have to say no, both Steve and Marcus said
it for her.

They guarded her like two dogs guarding a
sheep—even more fiercely than the parents with
their daughters, Cordelia thought wryly. But Steve

explained in a lull in the music, 'Sri Lankan men and women don't dance together like we do; they think it's more or less promiscuous. But the men have seen it on the American television pro-grammes and they go to all the night clubs hoping to get a dance. It really turns them on. If they can't get a girl they even dance with each other.'

When the music began again Steve asked her to dance. It would have to be Steve, of course, and not Marcus, but she smiled and went with him on to the small dance floor bathed in swirling, alternating bands of coloured lights so that the dancers had an eerie, ghostlike look. Cordelia immediately became aware of all the eyes on her, watching her every move. She wished now that she hadn't worn such a skimpy dress, had worn one with a back, with long sleeves even! She tried to lose herself, to forget everything except the music, but it was impossible; she wanted to keep turning her head to look at Marcus, to see if his eyes were among those that watched her. The dance came to an end at last and they went back to their seats. 'That was great,' Steve told her, his hand on her waist. 'I haven't enjoyed dancing so much since I've been over here.'

Cordelia managed to give him a smile of thanks, but she eagerly sat down again, hoping that Marcus would ask her next time. But he didn't seem in any hurry to do so and they sat and sipped their cocktails, using the swizzle sticks to search through the fruit and ice to find the liquid underneath. Another, extremely brave, Sri Lankan youth asked her to dance and didn't want to take no for an answer, then Steve stood up to his full height and glared at him and the poor young man melted away.

The band changed to a slower beat and Marcus touched her arm. 'Cordelia?'

She didn't look at him, just gave a small nod and walked ahead of him on to the floor. He put his arm round her and took hold of her right hand, lightly, not holding her close. Cordelia's head came about level with his shoulder, but she didn't raise it to look at him; she kept her eyes fixed on the collar of the silk shirt he was wearing where it opened to reveal the dark column of his neck. They danced slowly round the little floor. Occasionally someone brushed against her, but Cordelia wasn't aware of it, all she could feel was the touch of his hands, his closeness—and yet he was so very far away. She was very tense, her nerves felt as if they could snap at any moment. She wanted to be held close in his arms as she had been last night, to feel the warmth and strength of his embrace. Her hand trembled and she felt Marcus stiffen. Slowly she raised her head to look into his eyes. For a moment they were vulnerable and she could see the tension in his own face, then he had himself under control again and gave her a casual smile. But it was between them now, like a live thing, this emotion that he wouldn't allow to show, this desire that he had squashed before it could take fire. Neither of them spoke, the atmosphere between them was suddenly so charged that a word could have acted like a fuse. They danced on, but there might just have been the two of them in the room, so unaware was Cordelia of the people around them. She searched his face for some sign, some acknowledgment, but he wouldn't meet her eyes, again—like this morning—keeping his face as expressionless as a mask.

When they sat down again, Cordelia turned her attention to Steve, asking him questions about himself while the band took a break, and getting up to dance with him without hesitation when they came back. She danced with Steve the rest of the evening, they hardly left the floor except to take a drink. Marcus sat alone at the table watching them, a brooding look about his mouth, making no attempt to ask any other girl in the room to dance. At eleven-thirty he stood up rather abruptly and said, 'We'd better be heading back.'

'But it's early yet,' Steve protested.

'We've a long drive ahead of us, remember?' Marcus pointed out.

Steve looked to Cordelia to back him up, but she only said, 'I'll get my things,' so he was disappointed.

When they went out to the car she was worried that Steve might try to sit in the back with her, so she quickly yawned and said, 'I'm tired. Would you mind if I sit in the back instead of you, Steve, so that I can stretch out?'

He had to agree, of course; it would have been ill-mannered and obvious to have done otherwise.

It was a very fine night, the stars were out and looked like sparkling jewels against the warm, dark velvet of the sky. Strange stars, in constellations she didn't recognise. Cordelia lay across the back seat and watched them as they drove along. The two men were talking, the sound of their voices rolled over her, but she wasn't listening. If they had been talking about her, she might have done, but she knew they wouldn't do that. She could see the profile of Marcus's head as he concentrated on the road, outlined by the faint glow thrown up by the dashboard lights. What was he thinking? Cordelia wondered. Did he care about her at all? She would have given everything she had to know. But apart from that one moment when they had been dancing, he was like a closed book to her, she had no idea whatsoever of his true feelings, or even whether he had any for her at all. The car bounced gently along the rutted roads, for once quiet now, and Cordelia wearily closed her eyes, the motion rocking her into sleep.

She didn't waken until the car stopped and the lack of movement penetrated to her subconscious. Opening her eyes, she found that she was lying in a long bar of moonlight and that both men were looking over the backs of their seats at her.

'You're home,' Steve told her, adding with a clumsy attempt at gallantry, 'You look like the Sleeping Beauty lying there.'

Cordelia smiled and sat up, pushing her hair back from her head. 'So which one of you is going to kiss me and turn into a handsome prince?' she quipped lightly.

Marcus grinned. 'Are you saying that we're a couple of frogs?'

'We-l-l . . .' She raised her eyebrows expressively.

He laughed and got out of the car, opened the rear door and helped her out. After having been curled up in the back of the car for so long, Cordelia's legs felt rather stiff and it was a moment or two before she followed the men over to Steve's car. Steve had been saying something to Marcus in a low voice, but he broke off when she came over.

'You sure you won't stay the night?' Marcus said to him. 'You can doss down on the settee.'

'Thanks, but I've got to get back.'

'Goodnight, then.'

They shook hands and Marcus turned and walked towards the house. Cordelia, too, offered her hand. 'Goodnight, Steve. Nice meeting you.' She half-turned to follow Marcus, but Steve kept hold of her hand. Reluctantly she turned back to him, more or less knowing what was coming.

'Don't go in for a minute,' Steve said. 'I'd like to talk to you.'

'I'm tired, Steve. It's very late.' Cordelia glanced over her shoulder, looking to see if Marcus was waiting for her, but he had already gone into the house. Immediately she felt a stab of anger, guessing that Steve had asked him to leave them alone together.

'It won't take a minute. Look, I've really enjoyed tonight. I thought we might go out some other evening.'

'Yes, of course,' Cordelia agreed lightly. 'Whenever you and Marcus are both free.' She tried to pull her hand away, but he hung on.

'That wasn't what I meant; I meant just the two of us. In fact,' he went on with a rush, 'I've got a week's leave owing to me and I thought perhaps I could take you around the island. There are some places I haven't seen myself yet, like Adam's Peak, and we could do them together.'

'Thanks, but I really don't want to tie myself down. And besides, I promised to help Marcus with his book in return for his hospitality.'

'He won't hold you to that.'

'I know, which is precisely why I intend to keep my promise. He's been very kind to us, Steve. The least I can do is to help him in any way I can.'

He put his other hand on her waist and tried to draw her towards him. 'But I want to see you again, very much,' he told her thickly.

Cordelia held herself stiffly, not wanting him to kiss her. 'Look, I enjoyed tonight, it was fun, but I've only just met you . . .'

'Is there someone back in England? Is that what you're trying to say?'

'No,' Cordelia admitted. 'No one special. But that doesn't mean that I want to commit myself to—well, to being tied down. And anyway, you know about my father; he may want to leave here and go to a hospital as soon as he's well enough to be moved. I'm sorry, Steve, but . . .'

'All right, you don't have to go on; I get the message. I thought we hit it off okay,' he added ruefully.

'We did, and I like you. But I just don't want to get involved. Right?'

'Right. But if I phone or come over will you come out with me if you're free?'

With a little sigh, Cordelia nodded. 'But only as long as I'm free to say no if I can't.'

'Or don't want to.'

'That, too,' she agreed coolly.

Steve grinned suddenly. 'You're very determined, aren't you?'

'I like to be independent,' she corrected him. Pulling herself free of his arms, she said, 'Goodnight, Steve. Drive back safely.'

He didn't move immediately but watched her as she walked to the bungalow. At the door she turned and nodded to him. He lifted a hand in salute and climbed into his car. Marcus had already gone to his room; Cordelia went quietly to her own and listened to the noise of Steve's engine as the sound echoed through the quiet hills.

CHAPTER SIX

SUGIN came back the next day. Cordelia didn't sleep very well and got up early, looking forward eagerly to having breakfast with Marcus, but when she went out on to the verandah Sugin was standing by his chair, her arm along the back of it in a familiar gesture. Cordelia met the rather malicious look in the other girl's eyes and quickly looked away. 'Good morning, Marcus. Hallo, Sugin. How's your sister?' Somehow she forced herself to sound natural.

'She is much better now. How is your father?' The returned politeness mocked back at her.

'Coming along famously, thank you.' She sat down and poured herself some fruit juice, hoping that Sugin would go away, but of course she didn't. Smiling at Marcus, Cordelia queried, 'Work today?'

'Unless you'd rather take the car and go sightseeing.'

'You should go to Aukana,' Sugin put in. 'There is a statue of the Buddha there that you should see.'

'Thank you, but I've already seen the replica in Colombo, and I think I've had quite enough of doing the tourist bit for a while. I could do with a few quiet days,' Cordelia said firmly.

If Marcus noticed the battle between them he didn't show it. 'Good. I'd like to get on today.' He talked to both girls impartially until they had finished breakfast and then stood up immediately. 'Let's make a start before it gets too hot.'

122

Dr Matara came during the morning and said that her father was well enough to sit out on the verandah for a while each day. He also dispensed with the day nurse's visits, saying that Marcus's servants were quite able to see to the patient's needs now, but he went over her father's different medicines with Cordelia, making her responsible for seeing that he took them correctly. They took a break for lunch, but Cordelia said she wasn't hungry, instead putting on her bikini and finding a secluded patch of the garden where she sunbathed until it was time to get back to work.

Marcus was much the same as he had been before their trip to Sigiriya; friendly, willing to converse intelligently on any subject she chose, he even flirted with her a little once or twice, but he made no attempt to kiss her again and there was nothing behind it; he made sure she knew that.

After dinner they both went in to see James Allingham, but after a while the two men began to play chess. Cordelia tried to read a book but couldn't settle to it, so she excused herself and went for a walk in the garden, somehow feeling that neither man was sorry to see her go. Any faint hope she might have had of Marcus joining her died when she saw Sugin still in the house, her small, curvaceous figure outlined by the electric lights as she moved from room to room shutting the windows.

The next day passed very similarly except that Steve phoned in the early evening, before dinner. Cordelia was in her room and quickly slipped on a bathrobe over her underwear when Marcus knocked on her door. 'Steve's on the line,' he told her. 'Wants to know if you'd care to spend the evening up at the Expatriates Club.'

'Will you be going?'

He shook his head. 'I've promised to give your father a chance to get his revenge at chess.'

'Then I won't go either, thanks.'

'Why not, Steve will take care of you?'

'No. I don't want to go alone.'

A shadow crossed Marcus's face and he kept his eyes fixed on hers, as if willing himself not to let his eyes wander down to where her robe had slipped open a little and revealed the white valley between her breasts. 'How would you like it if we all went there tomorrow evening, then?'

Cordelia nodded and said a little huskily, 'Yes, I'd like that.'

'Okay, I'll tell Steve.'

When Marcus had said that they would all go to the Club, Cordelia had thought that meant him, Steve and herself; she hadn't realised that it also included Sugin. She went eagerly out to join him, looking forward to being alone with him on the journey to the dam site—and even more to the return journey home, but all her hopes fell ludicrously when she saw the Sri Lankan girl, dressed in a blue spangled sari, waiting in the hallway.

Trying desperately not to let her disappointment show, Cordelia smiled brightly and followed them out to the car. At least she got to sit in the front seat beside him, although Sugin's presence in the back, as quiet as Steve's had been talkative, was just as inhibiting. The drive to the dam site took about half an hour, but it was dark before they set off, so there was nothing to see. At this time of night the roads were still busy with people going home from work in the plantations and Marcus had to drive carefully, dodging the unlit bicycles and the transport lorries from the tea factories, loaded down with the people who were packed in far more closely than any cattle truck would be in Britain; at home, Cordelia reflected, if animals had been discovered packed in that tightly it would have made newspaper headlines and the whole country would have been up in arms!

They got to the Expatriates Club about eight-thirty and Steve was waiting to meet them. He immediately appropriated Cordelia for himself, taking her arm and drawing her into a big room where there was a bar along the whole length of the narrower wall and a largish space set aside as a dance floor. Tables were set out around the rest of the room and most of them were occupied. There seemed to be a majority of men in the room, all European in appearance, and Cordelia was surprised to see quite a few white women as well as several Sri Lankan girls.

At the moment when Steve escorted her into the room, there happened to be a lull in the music coming from a disco-type set-up over in the corner. They paused for a moment in the doorway, waiting for Marcus and Sugin, and all eyes seemed to turn towards them. Immediately Steve was the object of all sorts of comments, from the outrightly ribald to the plainly envious. It was obviously the sort of club where all the men knew each other so well they could be rude to one another without giving offence. Steve merely grinned goodnaturedly and led them across to an empty table. Cordelia sat down and found herself opposite Sugin, so she immediately turned and began to talk brightly to Steve.

As soon as the music started, Steve took her on the floor, introducing her to several of his friends as they danced. It turned out that many of the men she had taken to be European were in fact Australian, with one or two Americans among them. The white women were nearly all wives who had accompanied their husbands and who lived in small houses provided by the dam company, or girl-friends who were over on visits. None of the women were without a more or less permanent man, which made Cordelia the only really unattached white girl there. Steve of course made it known that he had first claim, as it were, but that didn't stop most of the other single men who hadn't got girls from coming over to be introduced. So Cordelia found herself greatly in demand and danced more or less non-stop. She was glad of it, not wanting to have to sit and look at Sugin's face all evening, a face that grew more disdainful as Cordelia let her hair down and really got into the beat. But Cordelia didn't care; she was enjoying herself despite Sugin's disapproval and Marcus's withdrawn coolness. He was sitting back in his chair, watching her rather broodingly as he drew on his cigarette. He didn't ask her to dance, but then he didn't ask Sugin either, no one did, although some of the other Sri Lankan girls were attempting to dance Western style, even though not very successfully.

There was a contrariness about Cordelia tonight. She looked at Marcus's dark features and thought, damn him, why the hell should I care about him? The man doesn't even know his own mind! She turned a laughing face up to the man she was dancing with and let him take her back to his table afterwards to meet some of his friends. She stayed chatting to them for about ten minutes, then Steve came over to claim her.

Later, after a particularly strenuous dance, Cordelia laughingly insisted on having a rest for a while. 'I'm exhausted,' she complained. 'I don't know whether it's the height, the humidity or the heat, but it really takes it out of you, dancing here.' She took a long pull at her drink and looked at Sugin. Rather recklessly she said, 'I notice you don't dance, Sugin. Don't you know how?'

The other girl's nose curled. 'Anyone can throw themselves about like that. That is not dancing. Real dancing is very graceful and has to be learned from a small child. Each dance is traditional and all the movements have to be learned. Throwing yourself about like a mad woman is not dancing.'

Marcus went to say something, but Cordelia broke in hotly, 'What you describe is professional dancing. In Britain we have a great deal of professional dancing—the ballet, for instance, which is far more traditional and graceful than your dancing; you have to be really good to dance in the ballet. But what I'm talking about is dancing by ordinary people for enjoyment. Do you know how to do that? Or do you only do it for money?' Cordelia added bitchily.

'Respectable girls would not dance so with a man,' Sugin retorted with equal venom.

'But we're not talking about respectable girls— we're talking about you,' Cordelia answered sweetly.

Marcus got to his feet, an angry frown between his eyes. Taking hold of Cordelia's arm, he pulled her to her feet and led her on to the dance floor. 'Why the hell are you picking on Sugin?' he demanded.

Cordelia bit her lip, realising how petty it must seem to him, but she couldn't tell him how

blatantly the other girl had tried to get rid of her.
'She doesn't like me,' she answered weakly.

'So what? You have every advantage that she
doesn't.'

No, not every one, Cordelia thought miserably.
She has you and I don't.

'And you know she can't get up and dance,'
Marcus was going on. 'It's against their custom.'

'There are other Sri Lankan girls here dancing,'
Cordelia said defensively. 'And there were quite a
few men in that night club in Colombo.'

'These girls are a lower class than Sugin. And
even then they wouldn't do it if there were any of
their own men around.'

'I'm surprised Sugin lowered herself to come
here at all if she's so high class,' Cordelia couldn't
resist remarking waspishly.

Marcus's frown deepened. 'She came because I
asked her to.'

He didn't explain why, which left Cordelia to
wonder miserably if it had been because he didn't
want to be alone with her during the drive, or just
because he preferred Sugin's company to hers.
And neither reason was very flattering.

The dance was a slow one and seemed to go on
for ages. She wished it was over. For the first time
Cordelia didn't want to be near him; she knew that
from his point of view she deserved his anger, and
the fact that it was in some way justified didn't
make her feel any better. She felt wretched and
just wanted to go home. But 'home' was the
bungalow where she would have to see both of
them together, knowing that they were lovers. She
longed suddenly to get right away, to never see
Marcus again. To go back to England and forget
that she'd ever met him, forget that one night

when he had taken her into the garden and kissed and caressed her—that one perfect night. She quivered and gave a half-sob.

Marcus's arm tightened round her waist. 'What is it?'

'Nothing.' She kept her head down.

'Cordelia?' When she did nothing he ordered, 'Cordelia, look at me.'

Slowly she raised her head, her eyes dark and vulnerable. Her lips trembled as she tried to control herself. Marcus's eyes met hers, searched her face. His lips moved and she thought he murmured something under his breath, but it was too low for her to hear. Turning her head away, she said stiltedly, 'I'm tired. Can we go home soon?'

'Yes, of course. Now, if you like.'

They went back to their table and he said to the others, 'Time for us to go, I think. Thanks for a great evening, Steve.'

'But you're not going yet! It's still early. Stay for a bit longer,' Steve protested.

'The girls are tired.'

'Cordelia isn't. Look, you take Sugin home now if she wants to go and I'll drive Cordelia home later.'

'Oh, no, that's far too much trouble,' Cordelia protested quickly. 'Thanks, Steve, but I'll go home with the others.'

'It's no trouble, I can easily . . .'

'Steve, I'd rather,' Cordelia told him sharply, her voice rising.

Catching the slightly hysterical note, Steve looked at her face and saw the strain in it. 'Okay. I'll see you off.' He walked with them to the car, hanging back so that he and Cordelia were behind the other two. 'Can I call you in a couple of days?'

Cordelia immediately felt remorseful for having snapped at him and nodded. 'Yes, that will be fine. Thanks for tonight, Steve.' She touched his hand in farewell, but Steve caught hold of her arm so that she had to stop. Turning her round to face him, he gave her a light kiss on the mouth. 'See you, then.'

'Yes. See you.' Cordelia went over to the car. Sugin was already sitting in the front seat and Marcus was standing at the back, holding the door open for her. Cordelia didn't know whether or not he had seen Steve kiss her; it wouldn't have mattered if he had, it was only a peck, but even so she was glad of the darkness that hid the flush that came to her cheeks.

It was Sugin's turn to become animated on the way home; she talked exclusively to Marcus, of people and places that Cordelia knew nothing about, shutting her out completely. When they got to the bungalow Cordelia said a hurried goodnight and went straight to her room, turning the handbasin taps full on so that she wouldn't hear them both going into Marcus's bedroom.

James Allingham was rather surprised at her solicitousness the next day. Cordelia went to his room first thing to give him his medicines and encouraged him to let the houseboy dress him after breakfast so that he could go and sit on the verandah before the sun got too hot. 'You're doing fine,' she encouraged him. 'You'll soon be fit enough to take a walk in the garden.' And then, she added to herself, you'll be well enough to take a car ride to the nearest hotel. Because all she wanted now was to get away from Marcus as soon as possible.

She worked nearly all that day. Marcus was

with her in the workroom for some of the time, but when her father came out on to the verandah he went to sit with him, leaving Cordelia to get on on her own. She typed very fast, wanting to get the job done with so that it wouldn't be on her conscience when she left. By the time she had finished that day the pile of beautifully clean typed manuscript had grown considerably and she was only a couple of chapters behind Marcus's rewritten and corrected draft.

Standing up, Cordelia stretched her shoulders, her back aching. The sun had started to set and she hadn't even noticed. Marcus came in while she was putting the cover on the typewriter and looked at the pile of typed sheets. 'You've done a lot today. You've almost caught me up.' She nodded and went to turn away, but he put his hands on her shoulders. 'You don't have to work so hard, you know.'

Lightly she answered, 'I don't like to be behind. Would you excuse me?' She tried to step to one side. 'It must be time to change for dinner.'

Marcus let her pass. 'Going out with Steve tonight?'

'No.'

'You seem to get on with him all right.'

Cordelia shrugged, her back to him. 'He's nice enough.'

'Well, don't feel that you have to stay here and help me if he asks you out.'

Biting her lip hard, Cordelia managed, 'No, I won't. Of course not,' then quickly escaped to her own room.

Seeing to her father's medicines and general wellbeing helped to take her mind off other things, and she also went to sit with him for a while in the

evening. Marcus came too and the two men again
played chess. Cordelia sat in a chair with her legs
curled up under her, a book in her hands, but
quite often her attention drifted from the pages
and she sat gazing broodingly at first Marcus, then
her father. After a couple of hours, Marcus went
to get some drinks and James Allingham looked at
her from under drawn brows. 'Is something the
matter?'

Cordelia raised her head in surprise. 'What do
you mean?'

'You've been watching the pair of us instead of
reading nearly all evening. If there's something on
your mind you'd better tell me.'

'It's nothing really, only . . .' she hesitated, 'only
I think it would be a good idea if we moved into a
hotel as soon as you're well enough to make the
journey.'

Her father frowned. 'Has Marcus said he wants
us to go?' he demanded bluntly.

'Oh, no, nothing like that. It's just that—well, I
think it would be a good idea, that's all,' Cordelia
said lamely.

'I suppose you're bored,' he said rather
peevishly. 'Well, I'm very comfortable, and I'm
being looked after far better than I would be in
any hotel. If you don't like it here you can
always go somewhere by yourself; I'm sure
Marcus wouldn't object—although I thought you
were supposed to be helping him with his book.
I suppose you don't like having to work, is that
it?'

'Not at all,' Cordelia answered coldly. 'I offered
to help him and I shall continue to do so until it's
finished. I don't want to take advantage of his
hospitality any longer than necessary, that's all'

After all,' she added tartly, 'he didn't exactly invite us here, did he?'

Whatever answer her father had been going to make was stifled as Marcus came back into the room. They started a new game, and Cordelia very soon said goodnight and went to bed.

By lunchtime the next day she had caught Marcus up on the book. He sat quietly at his desk, absorbed in his work and didn't notice that she'd stopped typing. She whiled away half an hour by giving the typewriter a much-needed clean, then went to persuade her father to join them on the verandah for lunch. She fussed around him unnecessarily, making sure that he was sitting fully in the shade, and also between Marcus and herself. He muttered once or twice about fussy women, but Cordelia noticed that he took full advantage of everything she did for him.

After lunch she changed into her bikini and went to sunbathe in the garden again. She chose a secluded place among the spice trees where the sun beat down on a clear patch of grass and slipped out of her sundress to lie down on the big, gaily-coloured beach towel she had brought with her. For an hour or so she did her back, feeling the sun soaking into her skin, then rolled over to do her front. The sun beat down on to her and she closed her eyes against the glare, but still it seemed to scorch through her lids. Vaguely she told herself that she ought to put on some more oil now that she'd turned over, but she felt too lazy and apathetic to do so. She let her mind go blank, wandering wherever it cared to take her, not thinking of anyone in particular, although it somehow seemed always to come back to Marcus. She dozed and woke, dozed again. The next time she opened her eyes Marcus was standing over her. At first he didn't notice she was awake because his eyes were on her body, slowly travelling its length, savouring its slim, taut beauty, examining her her as he would never have done ordinarily. Then his eyes reached her face and he saw her staring back at him. Their eyes met and held for a moment that seemed to stretch into eternity. His eyes, his face, were for that moment her whole world and nothing on earth would have made her break the spell. But presently Marcus's eyebrows flickered and he dropped to his knees beside her.

'You'll burn up if you don't put some of this on,' he told her, picking up the bottle of oil, his voice harsh, unnatural. Unscrewing the bottle, he poured some of the rich amber liquid into his hand and began to rub it into her shoulders, then down her body.

Cordelia wanted to close her eyes, to let sensuality take over as she savoured each stroke of his hands, but instead she kept them open, fixed on his face. His hands moved slowly, rhythmically, around the edge of her strapless bikini top, down each bone of her ribs and the inward curve of her waist. He didn't look at her face, just watched his hands working on her body, the oil turning the light down of fine hairs on her skin into spun silk. He seemed fascinated by what he was doing, his thumbs slowly outlining her hipbones, his finger-tips feathering along just under the edge of her bikini. Cordelia gasped, unable to withstand the sensations he was arousing in her any longer.

His hands stilled as he at last turned to look at her face. She gazed back at him, lips parted sensuously, the need to be loved large in her eyes.

But even though her eyes searched his face so intently, she couldn't tell his thoughts or his feelings, as always he kept them hidden behind enigmatic features. Huskily, on a note of heartfelt pleading, she said, 'Don't do this to me.'

His hands, that were still resting on her hips, moved involuntarily, tightening for a brief instant. Then he leant back on his heels and got to his feet in one swift, agile movement. 'Sorry,' he said laconically. 'But you need protection from the sun here.' Giving her a brief nod, he strode away through the trees.

Cordelia sat up and watched him go, thinking bitterly that she needed protection from him, not the sun. He had chosen to interpret her words as telling him to stop oiling her, but both of them knew that she had meant far more than that. Automatically she picked up the bottle of oil and finished off her legs, her hands unsteady. A pulse beat in her throat and she felt incredibly hot, but hot from the inside, not from the sun. Lightly she ran her hands over herself, remembering how *his* hands had felt, wishing now that she had let him go on, but part of her also fiercely glad that she had sent him away. She wanted now, more than ever, to get away from him. If he touched her again she didn't think that she would be able to bear it; she would do something crazy like taking the first plane back to England—or else telling Marcus that she loved him and wanted to go to bed with him. Either of which actions would lead to unbearable consequences. Which was why, when Steve phoned her an hour or so later and asked her to have dinner with him that evening, she accepted without the slightest hesitation.

They had dinner at the Hill Club in Nuwara

Eliya, the same place that Cordelia had visited with her father just before the accident. Steve called for her at seven, looking smart and different in a suit and tie, and looked at her feminine, lacy dress in admiring approval. 'You look beautiful,' he told her a little awkwardly, as if he wasn't accustomed to paying such lavish compliments. Cordelia smiled and thanked him, able to appreciate his approbation even if it did come from the wrong man. He was rather disappointed to find that she had been there before as he had wanted to surprise her, but Cordelia was as sweet about it as she knew how and she soon had him laughing and happy again.

He was an interesting man to have a date with, he had travelled a lot and had a store of good stories and anecdotes to tell. Ordinarily she would have enjoyed being with him, but more than once she found her mind wandering back to the bungalow and its occupants. Was Marcus playing chess with her father again tonight? Or was he devoting the evening to Sugin?

'So what do you think he said?'

Steve's question brought her back with a jerk and she managed to smile and shake her head. 'I've no idea. What did he say?'

'He said he found the panties hanging on a peg in the men's changing rooms at the rugby club!'

This was obviously the punch line of a funny story, and Cordelia wished she'd heard the beginning; it sounded intriguing.

They ate a beautifully cooked and served meal in the dining-room and afterwards danced to the music of a trio of Sri Lankans who played all the old American swing and jazz numbers of the thirties and forties; Glenn Miller and other big band tunes.

Music that sounded incongruous in that place and played by those people, and a far cry from the disco at the Expatriates Club, although Cordelia enjoyed it just as much, if not more, or at least would have done if Marcus had been there. Vainly she tried to push him out of her mind, to concentrate on Steve—after all, he was the one who was trying to give her a good time. But however much she tried to be nice to him, her heart just wasn't in it. He tried to draw her close as they danced and she smiled and allowed him to do so, but after a few minutes she moved away again, not deliberately, just from a natural reluctance to be held so closely by a man she didn't want. He tried to encourage her to talk about herself, but she told him only a little and then changed the subject, unwilling to give anything of herself to him except her company.

It was almost one in the morning before they left and Steve drove her back to the bungalow. 'How about coming sightseeing with me?' he asked her as they drew up outside. 'Will you be able to make it some time?'

'Yes, I can come tomorrow, if you like?'

Steve looked surprised and pleased. 'You mean later today tomorrow?'

Cordelia laughed. 'Yes. If you can get the time off from the dam.'

'That's no problem. I told you, they owe me some leave. Where would you like to go?'

'You choose.' She stifled a yawn. 'You know the places I've seen, so I'll leave it to you.'

'Okay. What time shall I pick you up? Would eight-thirty be too early?'

'No, that will be fine.' She put a hand on the door handle. 'I'd better say goodnight, then, so that you can get back and get some sleep.'

'In a minute.' Steve reached out and put a hand on either side of her shoulders, drew her back towards him. 'It's been great tonight, Cordelia. You're a wonderful girl.'

'Thanks, Steve, but I . . .'

Her words were cut off as he kissed her. She didn't stop him, and discovered that he'd been around quite a bit as far as that was concerned too. After five minutes or so, when he became more passionate and his hands started to wander, Cordelia drew back and said firmly, 'I'm going in now. I'll see you in the morning.' And she got out of the car at once, leaving him no chance of stopping her.

The house was very quiet as she turned the lights off behind her and went to her room. She undressed quickly, then remembered that she was meeting Steve at eight-thirty and that she hadn't got an alarm clock. The best thing to do, she decided, was to write a note asking to be called at seven-thirty and for breakfast at eight, and leave it where the houseboy would find it in the morning. Quickly she wrote the note, and then, confident that everyone in the house was asleep, walked out as she was, in pale blue shortie pyjamas, her face unmade-up, her hair brushed loose and swinging free about her head, to prop the note up in a prominent place where it was sure to be seen.

Not bothering to turn on the lights, she stuck her note on the handle of the kitchen door, but as she was coming back through the sitting-room, the door of the study suddenly opened and Marcus stood framed in the light shining through the doorway. 'Who's there?' he demanded sharply.

For a moment, Cordelia had a childish desire to bolt back to her room, but managed to overcome it and stay where she was, although her heart had immediately begun to race. 'It—it's me,' she managed. 'I'm sorry if I disturbed you.'

Marcus moved further into the room but didn't bother to switch on the light. 'Is something the matter?'

'No. I was just leaving a note for your houseboy to give me an early call in the morning.'

'You're going out with Steve again tomorrow?'

'Yes.'

'So you had a good time tonight?'

'It was all right.' It felt odd to be talking together like this in semi-darkness, the house silent around them. And the conversation was quite meaningless, just words; Cordelia was hardly aware of them. Her eyes were fixed on Marcus, standing tall and shadowed, his shirt open to reveal the long column of his throat, his sleeves rolled up above his elbows. Moving a little nearer, he said, 'Where did you go?'

'The Hill Club at Nuwara Eliya.'

Silence fell between them, a silence loud with the sparks of electricity that their physical need for each other generated. Then Marcus broke the silence by saying thickly, 'You look about fourteen years old, like that.'

'Do I? But I'm not.' Deliberately she moved a few steps so that the light from the study outlined her body through the thin material of her pyjamas. 'Am I?' she whispered.

'No.' The word seemed to be dragged out of him and he thrust his hands into his pockets as if he couldn't control them.

'Aren't you going to kiss me goodnight?' Cordelia asked huskily.

He stared at her for a long moment, then

answered by saying, 'I don't think that would be a very good idea.'

'Why not? You were willing enough to kiss me the other night in the garden,' she reminded him, an edge of hurt in her voice.

'Yes, I know. But maybe that wasn't such a good idea, either.'

Cordelia's eyes grew wide in her suddenly set face. 'What are you saying?' she demanded harshly. 'That you didn't enjoy what we did?'

'Oh, yes, I enjoyed it,' Marcus muttered, half to himself. 'Maybe I enjoyed it too much.' Seeing her distress, he moved closer and at last took his hands from his pockets and put them on her bare arms. Immediately a kind of electric shock ran through her and she quivered with emotion. 'That night—I think we both got more than we bargained for.'

'Is that—so wrong?' Cordelia gazed up at him, wanting to touch him, but afraid.

'For us—yes,' he told her, his voice suddenly becoming harsh.

Cordelia winced as if he'd struck her. 'But why? I don't understand. Don't you—don't you want me?' she asked desperately, her voice breaking.

'Want you?' His hands tightened and he said something under his breath, something that sounded like a curse. 'That has nothing to do with it,' he told her shortly.

'Doesn't it? I should have thought it had everything to do with it.' Throwing pride to the winds, she said, 'I know that I want you, Marcus. Want you very much.'

'Don't say that.' He took a step away from her. 'You're too young to . . .'

'Oh, for heaven's sake! I'm nearly twenty-one

years old. How old do you think one has to be to fall in love?'

He grew suddenly still and stared at her. 'Are you saying that you're in love with me?'

Slowly, her voice choking with emotion, Cordelia answered, 'Yes. Yes, I rather think I am.'

For a long moment he didn't move, didn't speak, while she waited in agony to see what he would do. Then, his voice harsh, grating, he said, 'Really? Or is it my job that you're in love with? The fact that there's some glamour and fame attached to me? Do you really think you'd have fallen for me so quickly if I hadn't been a writer?'

Cordelia gaped at him in stunned astonishment. 'But—but your job has nothing to do with the way I feel. It wouldn't matter what you did for a living, I'd still . . .'

'No? Have you even bothered to think about it?' He swung away from her, took a few paces across the room and gripped the back of a chair, his knuckles showing white. 'Okay, maybe you really believe that what you feel is love. But this isn't the first time this has happened to me, Cordelia. Young girls tend to fall for men in what they think are glamour jobs: actors, writers, racing drivers, pilots.' He smiled rather sardonically at bracketing himself with the last two. 'Then either the glamour wears off or else the man goes on to another girl. It's very nice for the men who take advantage of it, of course,' he added cynically.

'And have you—taken advantage of it?' Cordelia couldn't help asking.

'On occasion,' he admitted.

'But you don't feel like doing so on this—occasion?'

He turned abruptly. 'You're a guest in my house.'

She stared at him, anger mounting inside. 'So why didn't you think of that before you started—*flirting* with me?'

'Because I didn't expect things to get out of hand—or so quickly. I forgot that you were too young to know how to play that kind of game.'

'A game? Is that all it is to you? Oh, for God's sake!' She threw her arms wide in exasperation. 'What do you think I am—some infatuated teenager? I'm not, Marcus. I swear I'm not. What I feel for you is very real. Please believe me.'

His mouth thinned into a sceptical, mirthless smile. 'Isn't it time you got some sleep? *You don't want to keep Steve waiting in the morning, do you?*'

Cordelia gazed at him, her vision gradually blurred by tears, then she gave a helpless sob and ran to her room.

She was on time to meet Steve, for the simple reason that she had hardly slept all night. When he drove up she was already waiting by the front porch, a picnic hamper at her feet and sunglasses hiding the dark shadows around her eyes.

'Hi!' she greeted him brightly. 'I talked the cook into giving us a picnic lunch. Don't bother to get out. Here.' She handed him the hamper to stow in the back and climbed in beside him. 'How are you this morning?'

'Fine. And you?'

'Oh, great, just great. And raring to go. Where *are* we going, by the way?' she added as he reversed and then drove back down the driveway.

'I thought we'd go to Polonnaruwa. It's the other big ancient city. That's if it's okay with you,' he added anxiously.

'Sounds fine. Have you been there before?'

'No, it will be the first time for me too.'

Cordelia kept up an animated conversation nearly all the way so that she wouldn't have time to remember last night. She never wanted to think about the humiliation she had felt then as long as she lived.

The city with the unpronounceable name was nearer than the one she had visited with Marcus driving as a guide, so they had more time to spend there, but although Cordelia kept up the act of being interested in everything she saw, she soon came to the conclusion that one ancient city was very much like another. By midday they were both flagging and Steve suggested having their picnic under a tree, but this reminded Cordelia too vividly of a similar occasion with Marcus, so she firmly insisted that they go to a hotel where they ate their picnic sitting decorously at a table near the swimming pool while drinking cold beer from the hotel's bar.

Steve had a pair of trunks in the car, so he swam first to cool off while Cordelia leant back in a lounger and watched him. He stripped off very well, his body muscular and rock-hard, without an ounce of superfluous flesh. He showed off because she was watching him, diving in and then doing several lengths in a fast crawl, his arms cutting through the water and sending up a fine spray that glistened with the iridescence of cut crystal in the sun, each drop a prism of rainbow colours. As Cordelia sat and watched him, she wondered dispassionately whether or not to let him make love to her. That he would ask her some day soon she was quite sure; his kiss last night had told her that. All she had to decide was whether to say yes or no.

She wasn't in love with him, of course, that was for sure, and if she had sex with him that was all it would be—just sex, pure and simple. She might not even get any satisfaction out of it. Except the satisfaction of knowing that at least one man wanted her and found her attractive. And the intense, perverted sense of satisfaction at getting her own back on Marcus; because somehow letting Steve make love to her would be like aiming a blow at Marcus, even if she had to hurt herself to do it. I might even enjoy it, Cordelia mused as she watched Steve climb out of the other end of the pool and stand in the sunlight, legs apart, his hands on his hips. He waved to her and she lifted a lazy hand in return. He's obviously quite experienced and will probably be good in bed. He might even rid me of this frustration that's driving me crazy; make me able to live with myself again. Or even with him, she thought cynically. Maybe I'll like it so much I'll marry him and follow him from construction site to construction site all over the world.

Tears pricked at her eyes and she angrily wiped them away. Damn Marcus! I've done crying for him. But Steve wasn't Marcus and would never take his place. How could she possibly settle for anything less than love now that she had glimpsed it?

After lunch they dozed, then finished exploring the old city. On the way home they stopped at a seafood restaurant for dinner, Cordelia deliberately taking her time over the meal so that it was late before she got back. The next day Steve took her to the game reserve in the Yala National Park and the day after that to Galle on the south coast where they swam and sunbathed, wandered round

the town and had a very English tea on the
verandah of the New Oriental Hotel which,
contrary to its name, was the oldest hotel in the
whole of Sri Lanka.

Cordelia didn't even see Marcus during those
three days, making sure that she left before he was
around and going straight to her room when she
got home in the evening, only slipping in to visit
her father when she was quite sure he was alone.
But as she was leaving the house the next day,
Cordelia heard Marcus call her name. She
hesitated for a fraction of a second and then kept
on going, pretending that she hadn't heard him
and hoping to get outside to where Steve was
waiting before she had to face him. But the front
door hadn't yet been opened for the day and she
fumbled with the catches in her haste to get out.

'Cordelia.'

He was right behind her, there was no escape.
Slowly she turned to face him. His appearance
gave her a momentary shock of surprise: his eyes
looked tired and there was a bleak, pinched look
about his mouth. A great surge of emotion filled
her heart, completely choked her so that she
couldn't speak. She wanted to take him in her
arms, kiss away the lines around his mouth, make
him smile again. But then a small, cynical part of
her mind told her that he was only tired through
having sat up late, working on his book—or even
working on Sugin, it added masochistically. Her
face tightened as Cordelia answered coldly, 'Yes?'

'You're going out for the day again?' Marcus's
eyes went over her, lingering on her defiant mouth.

'Yes. Steve's waiting for me outside.' She turned
and reached up to fumble with the top catch of the
door again.

'Here, let me.' Marcus reached past her and slid the catch back easily, but in doing so his hand covered hers.

Cordelia trembled convulsively and jerked her hand away as if his had been red-hot. She couldn't move away because she was trapped between Marcus and the angle of the doorway, but she swung round to face him defensively, her blue eyes large and vulnerable in her pale face.

He gazed down at her for a moment, then said abruptly, 'I have an invitation for you. Sugin is appearing in an exhibition of Sri Lankan dancing in Kandy tomorrow night. She's given me a ticket for you; she thinks you'll be interested to see what traditional Sri Lankan dancing is like.'

'Does she, indeed?' Cordelia remarked sarcastically, knowing full well that the other girl merely wanted to show off her gracefulness and beauty, and in so doing make Cordelia feel gauche in comparison. 'Sorry, I have a date with Steve tomorrow.'

'He's invited, too, of course.'

'I really don't think it's his scene. Now, if you'll excuse me . . .'

She turned to open the door, but Marcus put out a hand and held it shut. 'Don't you think you owe it to Sugin to go? You were damn rude about her dancing when we were all up at the Expatriates Club last week. The least you could do is to go and watch her and see for yourself whether what she said was justified.'

'I'm really not interested. I . . .'

'Coward!' Marcus put in derisively.

Cordelia glared at him. 'I'm no coward.'

'Aren't you? Then why are you afraid of going to watch her dance?'

No good telling him the truth, of course; that all Sugin wanted was to show herself off and that Cordelia didn't see why she should waste her time and pander to the other girl's vanity by doing what he wanted. He'd never believe her anyway, she thought resignedly. This time when she pulled at the door she took him by surprise and got it open, hurrying outside, her high-heeled sandals clattering on the smooth stone of the porch.

Steve was waiting at the wheel of his car and looked surprised when Marcus followed her outside.

'Sugin wants us to go to Kandy to watch her dance tomorrow night,' Cordelia told him abruptly. 'Do you want to go or not?'

His surprised look deepened as Steve got out of the car to join them. 'I don't mind.' He looked at Marcus. 'Are you going?'

'Yes. I'll be driving the girls there.'

'Okay, then I'll come along.'

Cordelia shot a malevolent glance at Marcus; the way he'd worded it had made it sound as if she had already accepted. '*We* don't have to go if you don't want to,' she said pointedly.

But Steve didn't pick up the signal. 'No, it suits me. There are plenty of places in Kandy where we can go afterwards, if you'd like to eat there.'

Disgusted with them both and wanting to get away from Marcus, Cordelia got into the car and sat waiting, but the two men stood talking for several minutes before Steve finally strolled round and got in beside her. They spent the day in Colombo, but for Cordelia it was already spoilt. She sat silently in her seat and when Steve tried to talk she snapped at him, so that he gave her a wary, concerned look and left her alone. After an hour or so she managed to pull herself together a little and by lunchtime was outwardly back to normal, but the thought of the coming outing to Kandy hung over her like a black cloud the whole day. They spent some time wandering around the big, colourful market in Colombo, then went to the Intercontinental Hotel again to swim and have lunch. It was Sunday and there was a whole crowd of Sri Lankans round the pool, obviously richer better class people, from the clothes and jewel that they wore. They were mostly in family groups but there were a few girls there, wearing Western one-piece bathing suits, all of them slim and graceful, with large dark eyes and smooth olive skin.

Cordelia watched them playing around in the water, laughing as they splashed each other 'Steve, have you ever been out with any Sri Lankan girls?' she asked him.

He was lying on his stomach on the next lounge but raised himself on one elbow so that he could look at her. 'A couple of times. But the respectable girls are well chaperoned and the other kind just try and get as much money out of you as they can.'

'They're all very beautiful.'

Steve turned over and sat up so that he could see who she was looking at. 'Sure, when they're that age. They must be among the loveliest girls in the world. But then they get married pretty young have to work hard and have a kid every year, so that they're old by the time they're thirty. Have you ever seen any of them who're still beautiful over the age of about twenty-five?'

'No, you're right, I haven't.' Cordelia smiled at him, her heart oddly comforted.

'And none of them—but none of them, can compare to a certain blonde English girl I know.' And he kissed her right there in front of everyone, then grinned and pulled her into the pool for another swim.

That night Steve asked her to sleep with him. Not that he just came out with it like that, he used a far more subtle approach.

'How about going to Adam's Peak to watch the dawn rise?'

'I don't know. It might be fun,' Cordelia replied without a great deal of enthusiasm. 'You don't mean now?'

'No. Some other time. It's too late now. You have to get to the rest-house halfway up the hill in the early evening, eat and spend part of the night there, and then climb to the top of the hill just before dawn. There are guides with torches to light the way for you.'

'Why can't you just drive up there and then climb the hill?'

'The road is too dangerous at night, there are lots of hairpin bends. You have to get there in daylight.' He had stopped the car at the side of the road while they watched hundreds of tiny fireflies, and now he put his arm round her and kissed her. 'We could really make it a night to remember,' he murmured, his mouth against her neck.

Cordelia sighed and moved away. 'I don't know. I'll think about it.'

He tried to persuade her, but Cordelia wouldn't commit herself either way, and eventually he restarted the car and drove on through the darkness, the coconut oil lamps in the houses they passed casting a mellowing glow in the warm night. Cordelia gazed out of the window unseeingly, wondering why life always turned out to be such a mess. If it had been Marcus who had made that suggestion to her she would have been ecstatically happy, but with Steve—somehow it could only be sordid.

First the bad news, then the good news: unfortunately Steve had to work the next day and Cordelia was dreading having to spend the day working in the same room as Marcus, but when she eventually summoned up enough courage to go out on to the verandah the next morning, she found him dressed in a suit and on the point of leaving.

'I have some business in Colombo to attend to,' he told her, setting down his coffee cup. 'But I'll be back in time to take you and Sugin to Kandy.'

'Are there any more chapters of the book ready that I can work on?' Cordelia asked, carefully avoiding looking directly at him.

To her surprise, he said, 'It's finished. I've started typing it from where you left off.' He paused, then added, 'I thought you might not want to spend any more time on it.'

Lifting her head, she looked at him steadily. 'I said I'd finish it for you and I meant it.'

Marcus seemed about to say something, then changed his mind and nodded. 'See you later, then.'

He must have worked very hard while she'd been out with Steve, Cordelia decided when she went into his study and saw the amount he'd got through. If she didn't know better she could have believed that he had devoted all his time to it, all day and far into the night. She got to work at once and found some comfort in the familiarity of it, the need to concentrate to the exclusion of all else

By working solidly all day, she finished several chapters and left only a small pile to do—perhaps a morning's work.

They weren't having dinner at the bungalow that evening, there wouldn't be time before they left for Kandy, so at four Cordelia joined her father on the verandah for half an hour before going in to change. He seemed much better, able to walk around the garden a little, and spend as long as he liked outside, but his old restlessness seemed to have returned with his strength. Now he wanted to be completely fit again and was impatient with his own weakness.

At length Cordelia left him and went in to change. She put on a cream silk, sleeveless blouse and a matching straight linen skirt, with high-heeled sandals that looked good now that her legs were so beautifully brown. Even if I get nothing else out of this trip, at least I got a tan, she thought cynically as she checked her appearance in the full-length mirror in her room. She put on a minimum of make-up, just eye-shadows and lightener, mascara and a touch of lipstick, she really didn't need much when she was so brown, but her hair she washed and tonged into soft, loose waves around her head.

Marcus must have come home while she was changing, because Steve arrived about ten minutes before he put in an appearance. Steve was in his usual lightweight slacks and a casual shirt, but when Marcus joined them in the sitting-room where they were having a drink while they waited, he was wearing a collarless, short-sleeved white shirt and a native sarong covering his legs and tied in a knot at his waist. Cordelia choked over her drink and Steve burst out laughing.

'You're not actually going to wear that thing?'
he exclaimed.

'Why not?' Marcus answered, quite unperturbed.
'The hotel where the dancing takes place isn't air
conditioned and with all those people there it's
going to be damned hot, I can tell you. And these
sarongs are very practical in this climate. Why do
you think the natives in most hot countries of the
world wear them?'

'But don't you feel uncomfortable in it?'

'No. As a matter of fact it's a lot more
comfortable and cooler than trousers. You ought
to try it,' he added with a grin.

'No, thanks,' Steve said firmly. 'I just hope for
your sake it doesn't fall down. The native boys up
at the dam site seem to spend half their time
refolding the things and doing them up again when
they come loose.'

Marcus laughed. 'I assure you I won't embarrass
you.'

'Hey,' said Steve, going across to him. 'There's
something I always wanted to know. Somebody
told me that these sarongs are like kilts and they
don't wear anything underneath. Now, is that
true?'

'Wouldn't you like to know?' Marcus taunted
him. 'The only way you're going to find out is if
you get one for yourself. Then I'll tell you.'

The two men continued to rib one another for a
few minutes and then Sugin made her entrance.
She didn't simply walk in, but came to the French
doors from the garden and stood in the doorway,
the setting sun behind her, wearing a beautiful
golden sari with a little matching blouse which left
her midriff bare. Her face was heavily made up
ready for her performance, a great many bracelets

jangled on her wrists and she wore large earrings with green stones.

There was the hush she'd wanted as she posed in the doorway, and then she stepped into the room as Marcus moved to welcome her. He complimented Sugin on her appearance and Steve followed suit, then the Sri Lankan girl turned to Cordelia with a scarcely-concealed sneer, as if she expected the other girl to stay silent, but Cordelia, too, said, 'You look very—exotic. Very Eastern,' which Sugin didn't quite know how to take.

Marcus gave a thin-lipped smile as he watched the two of them. Coming across to take her empty glass, he said to Cordelia, 'And you look very Western,' which she didn't know how to take, either. Then he grinned at Steve. 'It seems we have the best of both worlds tonight.'

During the drive to Kandy, Cordelia sat in the back with Steve, and as soon as they got to the hotel where the display was to be held, Sugin disappeared round the back to change into her first costume. Cordelia had expected something rather grander than the big third-floor room with rows of old, hard wooden chairs set out in front of a stage that didn't have any curtains, the lighting coming from a row of primitive-looking electric lamps strung along the front. Tacked on the wall at the back of the stage was a big Sri Lankan flag with its angry, symbolic lion, but apart from this the stage had no other furniture.

A slim, very neatly dressed youth showed them to the seats that had been reserved for them in the front row. There were already quite a few people there, nearly all tourists, being escorted to their seats by couriers from the various package holiday companies, many of them complaining because they wouldn't be able to get a good view or didn't have a clear field of vision for their cameras. The performance was about a quarter of an hour late in starting and by then the room was very hot, even though all the windows were open. Cordelia wished she had brought a fan like some of the other women, but had to make do with the programme she had been handed as she came in and which listed the first item as 'Bolowing of the Conchshell: tradtional welcome and drum orchstra (By man).' And she could only hope that the music would be better than the spelling.

The first men came on in traditional dress, the notes of the drums differing because of the skins with which they were made; there was little tune to it and it was very repetitive, so that after a while it jarred on your ears. Sugin made her first appearance in a dance entitled 'Pooja Dance: Dance paying homage to the Buddha Doities and Guru (Dancing teecher) (By Girls).' There were three dancers, and Sugin was the middle one. They were all three equally graceful, beautiful and well rehearsed; Cordelia could well understand that they had to be taught the dances from an early age, for each movement of the body, of hands and of feet, was to a set pattern. It was interesting, it was very watchable, but to Cordelia it was too stylised, it lacked life and spontaneity, there was no emotion in it; the girls seemed to know the movements so well that they performed them automatically, their minds on other things, their eyes on the audience, gauging its reaction.

There were fourteen dances on the programme and by halfway through nearly everyone in the place was oozing with perspiration and longing for a drink, but all there was to be had was warm

Coke which you bought beforehand and which had to be drunk straight out of the bottle, without even a straw. Cordelia looked at the rust marks on the neck of her bottle and handed it to Steve, who took it gratefully. Marcus gave him an 'I told you so' grin; he was still cool in his loose clothing.

The programme was a long one, it lasted over two hours without a break, the hard wooden chairs growing harder by the minute. Cordelia shifted uncomfortably, hot and sticky, the discordant banging of the drums and the wail of the flutes grating on her nerves and giving her a headache. She longed for it to end, and even more for a long, cold drink. When it did at last finish with what was described as a 'Group Dance: perfomed by men and girls', the three of them, of one accord, headed for the bar on the ground floor of the hotel where there were at least a couple of electric fans to cool the place down. A youth in the doorway tried to take her programme back, but Cordelia hung on to it: its bad spelling and funny English had been the only highlight in the whole evening so far.

Steve bought her a cocktail with an arrack base; Cordelia downed it almost in one go. 'I needed that!' she declared fervently. Marcus and Steve both laughed at her vehemence. Looking up, she caught Marcus's eye and her heart jumped crazily, then began beating very fast. 'Do you think I could have another one of those?' she asked unsteadily. Sugin kept them waiting for nearly half an hour and during that time Cordelia had two more cocktails, the drinks acting on her empty stomach and going straight to her head. They ate in a nearby restaurant and had a fish curry, which was so hot that they needed several bottles of the local beer to cool it down.

'Here, sprinkle some shredded coconut on it,' Steve advised her. 'That's what the natives use to take the sting out of it.'

Cordelia looked round at the tables where parties of Sri Lankans were scooping their food up with their fingers, never having learnt to use knives and forks. She pushed her plate away. 'Thanks, but I can't manage any more; my mouth is on fire as it is!'

Sugin looked at her contemptuously. 'Your Western food is tasteless; you should use spices in your cooking.'

'If you've been brought up on curries like these, I'm not surprised that you find our food tasteless. I doubt whether you have any palate left at all. But then,' Cordelia added, 'we don't usually have to disguise the taste of rotten fish or meat.'

Steve had been about to eat a lump of fish, but now he paused, then lowered his fork and pushed his plate away. 'I don't think I want any more either.' Then he looked at Cordelia and they both burst out laughing.

They began to tell each other about all the worst foods they had ever tasted, vying with one another to find the most terrible. It was wicked to do so while the other two were still eating, but Cordelia didn't care; she felt in a reckless, frivolous mood and didn't much care what she said or did. They laughed uproariously over frogs' legs and sheep's eyeballs, and Steve knew of some really yeuky dishes which were so improbable that she accused him of making them up. By the time they left the restaurant she was giggling helplessly and in no mood to go tamely back to the bungalow.

'Let's go on somewhere,' she demanded. 'Surely there must be a night club or something here.'

'I do not wish to go to a night club,' Sugin said petulantly. 'I wish to go home. I am very tired after my performance.'

'We're all going back,' Marcus said grimly. 'Come on, the car's . . .'

'I said I'm not going.' Cordelia glared at him, rocking a little unsteadily but supported by Steve's arm.

'And just how do you expect to get back home late at night?' Marcus demanded, his eyes darkening with anger.

'We'll take a taxi—that's if we bother to come back tonight at all,' Cordelia replied shortly, her chin coming up in defiance.

Marcus took a furious step towards her. 'You don't know what you're saying. You've had too much to drink.'

'So what? What the hell has it got to do with you how much I drink?' she shouted, both of them now oblivious of the others.

'You'll do as you're damn well told!' Marcus reached out and grabbed her wrist, began to pull her towards the car.

'Hey, now wait a minute!' Steve put an arm round her waist and pulled the other way, so that she felt like a rope in a tug-of-war.

Marcus turned on Steve with a snarl that stopped him in his tracks. 'You keep out of this!' Then he glared at Cordelia. 'Are you coming, or do I have to pick you up and carry you?'

Ordinarily Cordelia would have thought before she spoke, would have hesitated before such anger, but now she was much too furious herself to care. 'No, I'm not!' she yelled at him. 'I'm going with Steve.' With a jerk she pulled her wrist free of his hand, then pointed derisively at his sarong.

'You've really gone native, haven't you? Well, why don't you just—just run along with your little native girl and leave me alone?'

Marcus's face twisted with rage and for a frightened second she shrank away from him as it looked as if he was going to do as he threatened, but then he swore savagely, turned on his heel and strode towards the car, Sugin hastily trotting after him with such a punch-drunk look on her face that it was almost funny.

Steve was equally astounded. 'What the hell was all that about?' he demanded as they watched the car pull away much too fast.

'I—I don't really know,' Cordelia muttered hollowly. She felt suddenly flat and exhausted, as if her blood had stopped flowing.

'I didn't know that you and Marcus were on the sort of terms where you could—well, that you disliked each other.'

'What? Oh, yes, we do. We—we can't stand one another,' Cordelia told him brokenly, her eyes still following the car out of sight.

Steve gave her a strange sort of look, as if he was seeing her for the first time all over again. 'We'd better go and find that night club.'

CHAPTER SEVEN

BUT they didn't find a night club. Instead they ended up at a hotel where several of the men Cordelia had met at the Expatriates Club were staying while on leave from the site. They were greeted uproariously and Cordelia found herself squashed on to a bench and a glass of beer put in her hand. The men had already had quite a lot to drink and were noisily and happily swapping experiences, telling jokes and singing. Some of the jokes would have made Cordelia's hair curl if they hadn't told her to cover her ears before the particularly rude ones. She sank with relief into the atmosphere, losing herself in it and glad to be just one of the boys for a while.

They broke up about three in the morning and Steve borrowed one of the men's cars to take her home. She was so tired that she staggered when she tried to walk and he had to help her out to it, and as soon as he got in beside her, her head slumped on to his shoulder and she fell asleep.

'Wake up, Cordelia, you're home.'

She sat up slowly and rubbed her stiff neck. Bright moonlight shone into the car. 'We're there already?'

'Yes. You all right?'

'Mm.' She yawned, but the sleep had done her good. 'Thanks for bringing me home. Shall I see you tomorrow?'

Steve gripped the steering wheel and said harshly, 'Is there any point?'

His tone made her look at him quickly. Her row with Marcus must have been very revealing, and Steve was no fool. Biting her lip, Cordelia looked away. 'No. I'm sorry.'

There was a minute's heavy silence before he said, 'Well, some you win, some you lose. But I would like to have won with you.' Leaning closer, he kissed her on the mouth. 'You'd better go in; I still have to drive back to the site.'

'I'm sorry, Steve,' she said again, but he merely gave a crooked kind of grin and reached past her to open the door.

Cordelia watched him go and then tried the front door. She wouldn't have been surprised to be locked out, but the door opened easily and quietly when she turned the handle.

Marcus was waiting for her in the sitting-room. He was sitting in an armchair, smoking a cigarette by the light of a single lamp, the ashtray beside him containing a small pile of cigarette ends. There was no newspaper or book in his hands to while away the time; he'd just been sitting there—waiting.

When Cordelia saw him she was immediately on the defensive. 'You don't have to say anything,' she said as he got to his feet. 'I'll leave here in the morning.'

'And go where?' Marcus bit out. 'Up to the site to live with Steve?'

'Where I'm going and who with is none of your damn business!'

A savage light came into his eyes as his temper exploded. He lunged forward, grabbing her arms and yanking her roughly towards him. 'Well, I'm about to make it my damn business!' And then he kissed her in a blaze of anger, hurting her deliberately, making her feel his strength.

'Let me go! You pig, let me go!' Cordelia twisted her head aside and tried to claw at him with her nails, but he pulled her arms behind her back and held her wrists imprisoned with one hand, using the other to grab a handful of her hair. Shaking with rage, he bent her against his braced body and forced her head back. Cordelia's mouth was open with the pain of his hold and her eyes blazed at him furiously. She hated him then, as she'd never in her life hated any man, and she began to struggle wildly, closing her mouth against him when he again tried to kiss her, her head jerking in a futile attempt to get free. His grip on her hair tightened so that she gasped in pain against his mouth, but still she kicked and writhed, even though she knew it was hopeless.

At last she quietened and he lifted his head to look at her. He was still terribly angry, she could feel it running through his body, see it in the grimness of his face. But now he knew that he had won and there was triumph too in his eyes. His fingers moved in her hair, turning her head into position for his last assault on her unprotected mouth. Slowly his head came down. He didn't close his eyes, but kept them on her until his hard mouth took hers and he opened her lips. Her surrender was complete; she hung limply in his arms, her strength drained away. Time seemed to stand still: he could have been kissing her for a minute or for an hour. Sound and sight had deserted her, she hung in a long black tunnel in which only the pressure of his body against hers was real. And it lit a fire deep within her that grew into an all-consuming flame. Her lips again moved against his, but this time in passion and need. He let go her arms and she slid them round his neck, clinging to him fiercely, wanting to lose herself for ever in his arms.

After a while, he bent and picked her up, carried her into her bedroom and shouldered the door shut behind them. They clung together for a long moment without speaking and then he gently took her arms from round his neck and began to undress her. He unbuttoned her blouse and slipped it off, and Cordelia shuddered as his hands touched her breasts, her hair tumbling round her neck. But her movement aroused him uncontrollably and his hands became urgent, as he took off the rest of her clothes, then his own, and lifted her on to the bed. He made love to her with a fierce passion that only became gentle and tender when his first hunger had been appeased. To Cordelia the night was a feast of rapture and she responded totally, as if the act of love with him was something she had waited for all her life. She yearned for him, ached for him, and only the mingling of their bodies in violent ecstasy could fulfil that need.

Afterwards, when he left her as the sun reached the pillows, Cordelia lay for a few moments in satiated happiness; she remembered the wide breadth of his shoulders, his weight as he pinned her to the bed, the salt taste of perspiration on his skin when she ran her tongue lightly across his chest. She recalled with joy how skilfully his hands had brought her to moaning arousal the second time and how much—oh, God, how much! pleasure his mouth could give. She tried desperately to stay awake, to go on reliving the night, but exhaustion drew her into the flowing stream of sleep.

It was late when she woke, the sun high in the sky. For a moment she thought that it was just a dream, but then she saw the bruise marks on her skin, felt the stiffness in her body. Quickly she got out of bed, wanting to lie and dream about the hours they had spent in making love, but wanting even more to see Marcus again, to touch him, to know that he was close. She paused while towelling herself dry to look at her naked body in the long mirror. There were bruises, too, at the tops of her legs and red marks on her breasts where he had been rough with her in his first hunger. Cordelia covered the marks with a pair of shorts and a bikini top, then hurried out to find her lover.

As she stepped out on to the verandah the sun caught her and she paused, lifting up her face to bask in it, stretching her body like a long, golden animal.

'If you go on doing that I shall want to do what I did last night all over again.'

Opening her eyes, Cordelia saw Marcus sitting in one of the padded garden chairs. A sudden shyness overcame her, but he held out his hand and she ran to him. Pulling her down on to his lap, he kissed her possessively. 'You all right?' he asked, when he at last released her mouth.

She nodded, her head on his shoulder, her blue eyes gazing lovingly into his. 'It must be very late.'

'Mm. Much too late for breakfast; you'll have to wait till lunch.'

'Oh, lor', I'm starving. Maybe I'll eat you instead,' she told him, beginning to nibble his ear.

Marcus laughed. 'You took several bites out of me last night. Wildcat!' he added, giving her a playful punch on the jaw.

Cordelia caught his hand and gently opened his fist, entwining her fingers with his, marvelling at its strength and size compared to her own. She felt that she wanted to look at him all over in the daylight, to memorise each hair, each pore of his skin, to know his body as well as her own.

'What are you thinking?' Marcus demanded.

'That I want to know every little bit of you,' she admitted, kissing his fingers.

'Do you indeed? And which part would you like to start with?' he asked suggestively.

But she refused to be drawn. 'Oh, your hand will do.' She paused, then added rather breathlessly, 'For now.'

His fingers tightened on hers and his eyes darkened. Pulling her to him, he kissed her again.

Neither of them was aware of the houseboy's presence behind them until he coughed tactfully. 'The post has arrived, sir.'

'All right. Leave it on the table.'

The servant withdrew as quietly as he had come and Cordelia sat up. 'He saw us.'

'Do you mind?'

She looked at him in some surprise. 'No—but I thought you would.'

'Why?'

She almost said because of Sugin, but she wasn't going to spoil the day by doing that. 'Why else did you leave me and go back to your room this morning?' she countered.

'Only so that you could get some sleep. Single beds may be okay for making love, but they're not very comfortable for two people to sleep in.'

'I wouldn't have minded.' She lay back against his shoulder again. 'I'd like to wake up with you beside me.'

He smiled and kissed the tip of her nose. 'Your father was out here earlier. He seems to have something on his mind.'

'He's had something on his mind ever since he came to Sri Lanka,' Cordelia agreed with a sigh.

'Won't he tell you what it is?'

'No. He's never confided in me. We're not very close—but then you know that.'

'Yes.'

They talked a little longer about her father and then Cordelia got off his lap while he looked at his mail and the servant prepared the table for lunch. After the meal they took the car and Marcus drove inland, away from the roads used by the tourist traffic. They stopped to buy a king-coconut for a couple of rupees from a pedlar and Marcus cut a hole with his penknife in the top of the big, bright orange fruit, and they shared the juice, the liquid trickling down their chins. Where the road petered out, Marcus parked the car and they walked along the bed of a green, sun-filled valley where wild flowers grew in profusion and streams from the high hills above hurried along their rock beds. They came to a place where a high ledge jutted out and formed a waterfall with a small pool below it. Here Marcus kissed her and slowly took off her clothes. His mouth found her breast and she held his head there and groaned with delight, never wanting him to stop, but he took off his own things and led her under the waterfall.

The water was stingingly cold after the hot sun and made her gasp, but Marcus held her against him until her skin was used to the change and she had stopped shivering. Then he began to gently wash her all over, exploring the while with his hands, his eyes, his lips, until Cordelia discovered that it was quite possible for fire and water to exist together. Then he took her, there under the waterfall, her cries of pleasure lost beneath the noise of the cascading waters.

It was the beginning of days of unallayed happiness. Cordelia found Marcus to be a wonderful lover, very experienced but willing to teach her, guiding her hands so that she would know what to do to give him pleasure, and appreciative when she learnt quickly or used her own imagination. They talked a little, they ate a little, but they were greedy for each other's bodies and spent most of the time making love. It was as if each time, instead of satisfying their appetites, only made them hungry for more, as if they could never have enough of one another. And each time was different; different in emotion and intensity. Sometimes Marcus made love to her slowly, taking his time, gently caressing each part of her until she couldn't stand it any longer and cried out for him to take her. Then he would tease her a little, pretending that he'd changed his mind, until she grew desperate and pushed him down on to the bed and *made* him love her. Sometimes he was like the first time, so eager and hungry for her that he took her with a demanding ferocity, his strength hurting her a little, and perhaps Cordelia liked it that way the best of all, because it was then, as his body jerked in uncontrollable climax, that he groaned out, 'Oh God, Cordelia. I love you! I love you!' He murmured endearments to her often, paid her compliments that frequently brought a flush to her cheeks, but they were the only times he said that he loved her.

They spent one morning working on the book until it was finished and then ceremoniously parcelled it up and took it to the post office to send to England. And, of necessity, they both spent some time with her father, but he seemed preoccupied and quite willing for them to leave him alone in the house. Marcus told her he had asked if he might use the phone, but they never saw him do so, so guessed that he must wait until they were out of the way.

'Did he say who he wanted to call?' Cordelia asked.

'No, but he asked for directories for the whole island.'

'How strange. I wonder what he's doing?' But Cordelia only puzzled over it for a few moments. When Marcus took her hand and led her into the garden she forgot about it completely. Just as she had forgotten about Sugin; the other girl hadn't been to the house since their first night together and she supposed that Marcus had ordered her to stay away. But after that first day she hadn't even thought about her, she was too high, too much living on a cloud to let unpleasant thoughts mar her happiness.

One day they got up very early and drove across to the eastern side of the island to the long, almost deserted golden beaches near Trincomalee, where the only shade was from the palm trees which grew on the edge of the shoreline. Marcus drove on past the beaches near the few tourist hotels until they found a small, secluded cove to themselves. There he insisted they take off their clothes, and Cordelia experienced for the first time the wonderfully free sensation of swimming naked, felt the warm blue water caress her body almost as sensuously as Marcus had. She also experienced for the first time what it was like to be laid down in the shallows and be made love to as the little waves rippled over them.

They lay close together on a huge beach towel, soaking up the sun, and Cordelia said dreamily, 'Will it always be like this?'

Marcus smiled and raised himself on one elbow, his eyes running over her nakedness in quiet pride of possession. 'Do you want it to be?'

'Yes. Oh, yes!' She spoke in a fervent, heartfelt tone, unable now to imagine any life but this.

'Then it will be,' he answered simply.

Cordelia thought about it for a moment and then sat up and looked at him. 'How, Marcus? What will we do when my father's well enough to leave here?'

'Don't let's worry about that now.' He lay back and reached up to caress her breasts. 'Why think about the future when the present is so perfect?' He began to pull her down on top of him. 'Come here, my beautiful, golden girl.' She smiled and without the slightest hesitation, did what he wanted.

The next night they dined at the bungalow and afterwards went for a walk in the garden. When they came to the frangipani tree Marcus again leant against its trunk, as he had that night when he had first kissed her with such passion, a night that seemed a lifetime ago. But now he brought it back by saying softly as he took her in his arms, 'Do you remember when we kissed under this tree—when we'd been to Sigiriya to see the Cloud Maidens?'

'Of course. I wanted you so badly. I thought you were going to take me to bed with you that night. Why didn't you? Didn't you want me then?'

'Are you crazy? God, you were driving me so wild that I near as dammit tore off your clothes and made love to you here on the ground!' For a moment his hands tightened on her arms, then relaxed. 'But it seemed wrong for all sorts of reasons. You were so young, and I didn't want to take advantage of you. And when you give, you give all of yourself—holding nothing back. Even that first time you spoke of love. But I wasn't ready for that sort of commitment.'

'So you decided to introduce me to Steve?'

'Mm.' He ran a hand absently through her hair. 'But then every time I saw you with him or thought about you together I got more and more jealous until it all blew up in my face and I couldn't stand it any longer.'

Cordelia laughed happily and put her arms round his neck. 'So you took me for yourself. It would have been a lot better if you'd done what we both wanted that first time. But you can always make up for it now,' she added, moving her thighs voluptuously against his.

His hands came down on to her hips. 'Are you suggesting what I think you are, Miss Allingham?' he demanded, his voice thickening.

'Oh, yes, Mr Stone,' Cordelia agreed breathlessly, feeling his body already start to harden. 'I am. Most definitely.'

'Well, in that case . . .' He laid her down on the grass among the fallen frangipani petals. 'No gentleman would ever disoblige a lady.'

It was much later when they crept back through the house to her bedroom, and the next morning, when he went to leave her, Cordelia clung to him and wouldn't let him go. 'Please stay with me,' she begged.

'I have an appointment with the bank in Colombo,' he reminded her.

'But you don't have to leave yet,' she coaxed. 'Just one more time.'

'He laughed. 'Woman, you're insatiable!' But he lay back beside her.

'Oh, Marcus, I love you. Is it wrong to want each other so much?'

'Wrong? Of course not. My darling girl, you're one in a million. The kind a man dreams of all his life but only a few are lucky enough to find: beautiful, sexy and intelligent.'

'Am I really sexy?'

He looked at her in mock seriousness. 'Perhaps, madam, you would like me to demonstrate yet again just how sexy I find you?'

'Oh, yes,' Cordelia agreed fervently. 'Yes, please!'

When they finally woke, cramped together in the narrow bed, the sun was already high in the sky. Marcus groaned and looked at his watch. 'My God, look at the time! Where the hell are my clothes?' He found his trousers and pulled them on, then turned to kiss her. ' 'Bye, darling, see you later. Lord, I wish I didn't have to go,' he added softly as he gazed down at her languorous eyes, her golden hair forming an aureole around her head.

'Don't, then. Stay with me,' she murmured.

'Jezebel! But I'll soon be back.' He kissed her again and Cordelia lifted his hand to her breast. He caressed her with growing passion, then with an oath tore himself away and went into the bathroom to shower. She smiled and lay there contentedly, drifting off to sleep again after she heard his car drive away.

She slept for another hour or so and woke feeling on top of the world, jumping out of bed and already counting the hours until Marcus would return. What would they do today? she wondered. Maybe they'd go to the famous botanical gardens in Kandy, a trip Marcus had promised her for some time. But there were bound to be lots of people there and they wouldn't be able to make love for hours and hours, so maybe they wouldn't go there after all. Cordelia laughed happily and whistled a tune as she showered and washed her hair. Putting on a bathrobe, she went back to her bedroom—and stopped dead in her tracks. Sugin was in the room, standing by the bed.

After a stunned moment, Cordelia burst out, 'What are you doing here? Get out of my room at once!'

But the other girl didn't answer, just stared at her stonily, and then Cordelia saw that she was holding Marcus's shirt. It had a grass stain on it where they had made love in the garden last night; that, and the tumbled bed, told their own story.

After a long moment in which Cordelia just looked at her helplessly, Sugin broke the silence by saying bitterly, 'So he is your lover. That's why he told me not to come here any more.'

'I'm sorry,' Cordelia answered inadequately. 'But, you see, we love each other and . . .'

Sugin's harsh laughter cut off her words. 'Love? You really think he loves you, you stupid English girl? He takes you only because you're easy, cheap. Because you will give yourself to any man who wants you.'

'How dare you?' Cordelia demanded furiously. 'Get out of here. Do you hear me? Get out of this house!'

But Sugin faced her obstinately. 'You cannot

order me to do what you want, English girl. You are not the mistress here and never will be.'

'Not yet, maybe,' Cordelia retorted angrily. 'But when Marcus and I are married, I'll . . .'

'Married?' Sugin laughed spitefully. 'Do you really think that he intends to marry you?'

'Yes. Yes, I do,' Cordelia replied without hesitation, but rather taken aback by Sugin's vehement tone.

Jeeringly the other girl went on, 'He will never marry you, English girl. How can he—when he already has a wife?'

The room seemed to go suddenly cold and fade away around her so that Cordelia could see nothing but Sugin's spiteful, jeering face. 'I don't—I don't believe you,' she said dully.

'No? Then I'll prove it to you. Come.' She led the way into Marcus' bedroom, a room in which Cordelia herself had only been in to once or twice, and then only for a few moments while Marcus was there. Sugin went straight over to a small desk and opened the right-hand lower drawer, took out a bundle of letters and shoved them at Cordelia. 'See, the address on the back. From Mrs Annette Stone.'

'They could be from his mother,' Cordelia said faintly. 'Or—or a sister-in-law.'

'He has no mother. Or any brothers,' Sugin told her viciously. 'Don't you even know that about him yet? You still don't believe me? Come, I'll show you.' She took Cordelia's unresisting wrist in a rough grip that hurt and pulled her into the study. 'Look.' She went to an old unmarked box file that was lying on a bottom shelf and that Cordelia hadn't ever noticed before. Inside were some old notepads and a scrapbook of press cuttings and book reviews. Sugin quickly turned the pages of press cuttings and stopped at a photograph. 'There!' she said triumphantly.

The photo was dated seven years ago and showed a younger Marcus without the sardonic lines around his mouth. He was smiling happily down at the girl who stood beside him; a slim, dark-haired girl who was laughing excitedly, her eyes on the camera. The caption under the picture said, 'Marcus Stone, whose latest book *The Gateway to Hell* has just sold a million copies, with his wife Annette at the Foyles' Literary Lunch given in his honour'.

The world seemed to explode into a grey mist through which she had to grope her way, but somehow Cordelia found herself back in her own room, alone, and with the door locked behind her. She sat there, huddled into a chair for a long time, then numbly got up, dressed and packed her clothes.

James Allingham was sitting at a table in his room when she knocked and went in to see him. He had several papers spread out before him, together with a map of the island. He looked up with a frown, then saw her white face and said, 'Is anything the matter?'

'Yes. I'm leaving here,' Cordelia answered baldly.

'Why?'

'That doesn't matter. I'm going back to England.'

'I'd rather you didn't. Cordelia, there's something I want to tell you. It's about why I wanted to come out here.'

Cordelia stared at him. 'You want to tell me that now?' she demanded angrily. 'Now? After all

this time? Well, I'm not interested. I'm going back
to England.'

'Please.' He looked at her in some distress. 'Has
something happened between you and Marcus? I
couldn't help noticing that you were—well, very
friendly.'

Cordelia nodded, unable to put it into words.
'And now I just want to get away from here.'

'All right, but will you please stay in Sri Lanka?
Just for a short time. I shall be well enough to
leave here soon. There's something I have to do,
something I've already put in hand, and then we'll
be able to travel back together, although it will
probably have to be by sea.'

'All right,' Cordelia agreed, quite indifferent to
where she went. 'I'll phone you when I find
somewhere.'

He gave her some money and she left him,
cutting him short when he again tried to tell her
his reasons for coming to Sri Lanka. The taxi she
had ordered arrived soon after and she left without
any fuss, not even looking back to see if Sugin was
triumphantly watching her departure. She told the
driver to take her to Negombo on the west coast, a
highly popular tourist area where she could lose
herself among all the other Europeans. The road
was the same one that led to Colombo, and after
they had been driving along it for an hour or so
she recognised Marcus's car going in the other
direction, back to the bungalow. He was driving
fast and there was an eager, expectant look on his
face.

Cordelia leant back in her seat and he didn't see
her, was too impatient to get home to look into
passing cars. But what a surprise he would get
when he arrived and found her gone. He would

just have to make do with his native girl again until some other gullible fool came along, Cordelia thought with bitter cynicism.

CHAPTER EIGHT

CORDELIA booked into one of the tourist hotels just outside Negombo without any difficulty and went straight to her room. It was much hotter here on the coast than in the hill country, but the room was air-conditioned and felt reasonably cool. She didn't bother to unpack or anything, but just lay down on the bed and gazed up at the white-painted ceiling. She must, she supposed, have been incredibly stupid, but it had honestly never occurred to her to wonder if Marcus was married. He had never spoken of a wife, of a family. Had he any children? No, if he had Sugin would have been bound to taunt her with that too.

She'd been such a fool! But she loved him so much. The thing that hurt most of course, was that he hadn't been honest with her, hadn't told her himself that he wasn't free. She had given herself to him so eagerly, so trustingly, certain that what they had was so strong that nothing could break it, that they would be together for ever, and now she felt that her trust had been betrayed. She had taken it for granted that she and Marcus would marry, when her father was better, when they all went back to England. There hadn't been any feeling of urgency; the world was standing still for them and the 'now' was so perfect that the future was too far away to even think about. He hadn't said that they would marry in so many words, of course, but there hadn't been any need to, it had been explicit in his eyes, his touch, his

lovemaking. And he *had* said that it would go on
for ever; wasn't that the same as saying that they
would spend the rest of their lives together? But he
hadn't meant it, must have been lying through his
teeth just to keep her sweet. Miserably Cordelia
turned her head into the pillow and wept.

She stayed in her room all that day and most of the
next, either out on the balcony or on the bed, but by
the evening of the second day she began to feel giddy
and realised that she would have to go down and eat.
Red-clothed tables were set out on the open terrace
only ten yards or so from the beach and there was a
cool breeze from the sea. A trio of Latin-American
singers moved among the tables, playing the guests'
requests on their guitars. Cordelia was given a table
to herself and ordered some food, forcing herself to
eat it. The waiters, all slim and young, seeing that she
was alone, tried to persuade her to go to the night
club in the hotel that evening, but she just shook her
head silently and they left her alone.

After the meal she went back to her room and
picked up the phone, hesitated a moment, then
dialled the number for the bungalow. Marcus's
voice answered and wrenched her heart so cruelly
that for several moments she couldn't speak. He
repeated the number and she managed to say,
'James Allingham, please.'

'Cordelia! Cordelia, is that you?' Marcus
demanded sharply.

'I want to speak to my father.'

'Cordelia, where are you? You *must* tell me!'

With a sob, she slammed the receiver back on its
rest, unable to take any more.

She tried to phone again, an hour or so later,
and this time the houseboy answered. 'Mr
Allingham, please.'

After a short wait her father came on the line. 'Hallo.'

'It's Cordelia. I've booked into a hotel near Negombo.'

'What's it called?'

'Brown's Beach. But don't tell Marcus.'

'Very well, if that's what you want. Are you all right?'

'Yes. How are you?'

'Oh, progressing.' But he sounded tired. 'Look,' he added rather awkwardly, 'Marcus is here. He'd like to speak to you. He wants to know why you left. It seems you didn't leave him a note or give any explanation before you went.'

'No. I don't want to speak to him.'

'But I really feel that you owe him that much.'

'No! I don't owe him anything!' Cordelia retorted vehemently.

'But he's been very kind to us. I don't have to remind you of that. Won't you at least speak to him—tell him why you left?'

'No. I won't speak to him. But you can—but you can ask him how his wife is.' And then she put down the phone, her hands trembling so much that she almost dropped it.

Cordelia spent all the long, hot days close to the hotel, only leaving it to take solitary walks along the endless golden beach, her bare feet sinking into the wet sand and making footprints that were immediately wiped away by the next wave. Most days she went out to the pool to swim and sunbathe on a lounger, her skin becoming darker as her hair bleached to a lighter shade of gold. Sometimes a man would try to pick her up, but he had only to look at the desolation in her eyes to know that it was hopeless and turn and go away.

At the weekend she saw two faces that she knew: men from the Expatriates Club who were friends of Steve's. Cordelia managed to avoid them, but she wasn't sure whether or not they'd seen her. Not that it mattered—nothing mattered now.

Every day she expected the promised phone call from her father, and as the days passed and lengthened into a week she began to wonder if he was having difficulty in finishing the business he had said he had still to do here. She wished now that she had listened when he was going to tell her what it was. Often her eyes went to the phone as she wondered whether she ought to call him again. But she was afraid that Marcus might answer and so she left it, telling herself that he must ring soon.

Then, one evening, at about nine o'clock, there was a knock on her door. Cordelia had already been down to dinner and was sitting on the balcony, her eyes closed, listening to the sound of the waves pounding on the shore and above it the music from a band of musicians who were playing for all the people who were still eating down on the terrace. She was wearing a turquoise-blue halter-neck dress with a full soft skirt, not because she had chosen to wear it but because it was the first thing that came to hand. The knock came again and she reluctantly got up to answer it, thinking that it was the maid who came round every evening to spray the room with insecticide to kill any mosquitoes that might have got in during the day. Pulling back the bolt, she opened the door and began to say, 'Okay, you can . . .' then stopped dead, frozen with shock.

Marcus stood in the doorway, a hard, set look on his face. Before she had recovered enough to move, he strode into the room so that she had to

move backwards to get out of the way. Then he
shut the door firmly behind him.

'What—what do you want? We have nothing to
say to each other.' Cordelia's hands were
trembling and she had to ball them into tight fists
in the hope that he wouldn't see.

'On the contrary, I have a great deal to say to
you,' Marcus told her grimly. 'But it will have to
wait. Right now, I'm afraid I have some bad news
for you.'

'Bad news?' Cordelia saw in his face a mixture
of seriousness and compassion and knew at once
that her father had died. 'Oh!' For a moment she
couldn't take it in, then she said on a note of
protest, 'But he was getting better! He said he'd
soon be well enough to go home.'

'He was. But yesterday he wanted me to take
him—he wanted to do something before he left,
something that involved quite a long car ride. I
didn't want him to, but he insisted. He was all
right, or he seemed to be, but later on, in the
evening, he had another heart attack and he died
early this morning.'

Cordelia slowly sat down on the bed. 'Did he—
do what he wanted?'

'Yes.'

'I'm glad.'

She sat silently for several minutes while Marcus
stood watching her, then he said, 'The funeral has
been arranged for tomorrow.'

'So soon?' But then she remembered that in this
hot climate funerals had to take place quickly.
'Yes, of course.' She tried to gather her wits.
'Where?'

'In Nuwara Eliya. There's a Protestant burial
ground there.' He looked at her for a moment

and then round the room. 'Shall I help you to pack?'

Cordelia stared at him stupidly. It still hadn't sunk in that her reason for staying here was gone, that she no longer had anyone to wait for. 'But you said the funeral wasn't till tomorrow.'

'No, but I'll take you back with me now. There won't be time for you to travel out there tomorrow.' Crossing to the wardrobe, he took out one of her suitcases and put it on the other bed, began to pack some of her things into it.

'Wait—I can do that myself.' But he insisted on helping her, and almost before she knew it, Cordelia found herself at the desk, paying her bill and checking out.

As they drove along she realised that Marcus had hurried her deliberately, giving her no time to think, but now she had to face the fact that she was going to be alone with him at the bungalow again, unless ... She turned to him, 'Is Sugin still—with you?'

'If you mean is she at the bungalow, then no. She's gone to live with her sister—for good.'

'You mean she isn't coming back?'

'No. And she never was with me—in the way that you mean,' he added tersely.

They were both silent then for several miles until Cordelia said with difficulty, 'My father was going to tell me his reasons for coming here, but at the time I—I wasn't very interested. Did he tell you, then, what they were?'

'Yes, he did.' Cordelia waited expectantly, but after a pause Marcus went on, 'I think perhaps it would be better if I left the explanations until tomorrow. It's a bit complicated.'

'All right.'

They lapsed into silence again, but it was a restless silence which lay between them like a tangible thing. They had been so close but were now so far apart, neither of them willing to speak about what had happened and release the flood of words and emotions it would bring. Now was not the time nor the place—for Cordelia there would never be one, so they both stayed silent during the long drive through the night.

When they got to the bungalow, the houseboy opened the door as soon as the car drew up and gave her such a warm and sympathetic greeting that for the first time she felt close to tears. He took her cases out of the car and carried them into her old room. Cordelia opened her mouth to protest, but then realised that there was no alternative. Marcus was looking at her questioningly, so she quickly turned and went into the sitting-room. He followed her and closed the door. 'Would you like a drink?'

She shook her head and went to sit in a chair that had its back to the garden, her hands gripped together tightly in her lap. 'Is my father—is he still here?' she asked with difficulty.

'No. His body has been taken to Nuwara Eliya. Do you want to see him before the funeral?'

'No. Oh, no,' she said hastily, recalling how she had been taken to see her mother after she died and could never then remember her alive.

'Very well.' Marcus poured himself a drink and sat opposite her, his face dark and shadowed, making the lines around his mouth appear deeper than they had been. 'Is there anything else you want to know?'

'Did he—tell you where I was staying?'

'Yes, towards the end. I'd begged him to tell me before, but he wouldn't—not until after he had the heart attack and knew he would never be going back to England. Then he told me.'

The bitterness in his tone made her quickly glance at him, but his eyes were fixed on her so she looked away again, her heart beginning to beat faster. If he had begged her father to tell him where she was he must have wanted to see her quite badly. She swallowed and changed the subject. 'You said he told you why he came here?'

'Yes.' Marcus looked down at the glass in his hand, swirled the liquid in it, as if he was trying to make up his mind, then he said, 'Did your mother ever tell you why she left your father?'

Cordelia lifted her head in surprise. 'She didn't actually leave him—she just couldn't take the climate here.'

'That may have been what you were told at the time, but—according to your father—it wasn't the real reason.'

'What do you mean? What was the reason, then?'

'It seems that your father had an affair with a local girl, the daughter of one of the workers on the tea plantation. It lasted for some time and was quite serious—so serious that he asked your mother for a divorce, but she wouldn't give it to him. Instead she tried to break up his affair, but when that didn't work she sent you to England and later cleared out herself. Your father admitted that the whole thing was his fault, entirely his fault, but he was infatuated with this girl. And,' Marcus went on slowly, his eyes fixed on her stunned face, 'there were two children of their—liaison.'

'Two children?' Cordelia stood up agitatedly. 'I can't believe it! Why didn't my mother tell me?'

'Possibly because she didn't know. I gather that the children were born after she left, but then the mother died and it was thought best for them to be brought up by her brother, who adopted them as his own.'

'But they're still here—in Sri Lanka?'

'Yes. Of course your father had to leave when the tea plantations were nationalised. He sent them money from time to time, but then the family moved and he lost touch with them. That's why he wanted to come back here—to find them and to make sure that their future was secure.'

'I see.' Cordelia sat down on the edge of a chair. 'And he found them all right?'

'Yes. He contacted people he used to know here and with their help managed to find them. Then he arranged with a solicitor to settle some money on them. That was where I took him yesterday—and to see the children.'

'Do they know he's their father?'

'No.' Marcus shook his head. 'And it was his wish that they never would.'

'But I don't understand why he brought me here with him.'

Marcus got up and poured himself another drink, then glanced at Cordelia a moment and filled another glass. He handed it to her and she took it automatically, looking at him enquiringly. 'The settlement was part of his will. As his next-of-kin you were bound to find out about it. Also it meant that he would have less to leave you. He wanted to explain to you about that, and I think he felt he could do that best if you were here and could see for yourself how poor the people are.'

'Was he afraid that I'd contest it or something?'

Shrugging, Marcus said, 'I don't know. I think he just wanted everything to be in order before he died.'

'But coming here and putting things in order killed him,' Cordelia pointed out. 'Why couldn't he have told me from the start?'

'Maybe he was afraid that you'd react like your mother and have nothing to do with him.'

'Was he? I'm surprised he even bothered with me when it was his other family that he loved,' she said bitterly.

'But he loved you,' Marcus told her earnestly. 'Otherwise he would never have stayed with your mother so long. He told me that the marriage had been unhappy from the start. And, believe me, there's no point in trying to hold together a marriage that's fallen apart,' Marcus said heavily, his voice sounding strange.

'He could have come to see me,' Cordelia said unhappily. 'He could have written.'

'He told me that he wanted to, but your mother wouldn't let him. And then after she died your aunt just took you over, and you were so cold and distant towards him that he thought he'd lost you.' He paused, but when she didn't speak, added, 'Perhaps he hoped that you would get to know each other again while you were here.'

Cordelia laughed harshly. 'That's ridiculous! You saw how he was. He never once made any— any offers of reconciliation, if you like. Quite the opposite. He was almost always brusque and short with me.'

'Maybe he didn't know how. He was a proud man, Cordelia. Maybe he could have used some help from you.'

Cordelia stiffened and put down her glass. 'You seem to have got to know him extremely well,' she remarked sarcastically.

'Yes, I did—after you ran away. We spent a lot of time together—when I wasn't scouring every hotel in every town I could think of, trying to find you,' Marcus said grimly.

Cordelia's face paled. She stood up, a little unsteadily. Marcus put a hand under her elbow, but she jerked her arm away. 'Don't touch me!' she flared angrily.

His face darkened and for a moment she thought he was going to force the issue, but then he stepped back. 'You're tired,' he said curtly. 'You'd better go to bed. We'll talk tomorrow.'

She glared at him for a moment, then suddenly all defiance left her, so she just nodded and went to her room. But just walking into it brought back so many memories; memories of the most ecstatic lovemaking, of words said, of caresses exchanged. In a semi-automatic state, she washed and changed into pyjamas, but it took a sheer effort of will to get into bed and turn off the light. And then she lay there, in the bed they had shared so often, knowing that Marcus was only a few feet away, her body crying out for him, and the memories came and engulfed her so that she lay awake far, far into the night.

To Cordelia's surprise there were quite a lot of people at the funeral. Many of them introduced themselves as friends of her father from his tea plantation days, and she guessed that these were the people he had contacted to help him find his other family. All of them said they remembered her as a child, so that she was touched and grateful to them. They all came back to the bungalow to lunch afterwards, and as several of them knew who Marcus was, he was kept busy answering questions about his work.

It was gone three before the last one left. Cordelia politely shook hands with them and watched their car until it turned out of the gate, then gave a sigh of relief and immediately turned and hurried inside the house.

'Cordelia!'

Marcus called after her, but she took no notice, going straight to her room and locking the door. Quickly she changed out of the black and white dress which was the only suitable thing she had had to wear, and put on a short-sleeved shirt and a pair of jeans. The rest of her things she packed and closed the cases. Then she went to the door, her hands trembling, and turned the key.

He was waiting for her, of course. She had known that there was no way he was going to let her leave without facing him. He took one look at her clothes and the cases and anger flamed in his eyes.

'And just where the hell do you think you're going?'

'Home. Back to England,' Cordelia replied steadily.

'You're not going anywhere. You and I have some talking to do,' he told her grimly.

'No, there's nothing to say. May I use your phone to call for a taxi, please?'

'No, you damn well may not!'

'All right, then I'll walk.'

She bent to pick up her cases, but Marcus swore and wrenched them out of her hands, then he grabbed her wrist and pulled her after him as he strode through the house and out into the garden, almost making her fall down the steps as he dragged her along.

'Stop! Let me go!' Cordelia tried to pull away, but he hauled her along until they were well away from the house. Then he swung her round to face him.

'Now perhaps you'll tell me why you ran away without even bothering to leave a note?' he demanded with scarcely controlled violence.

'You know darn well why.' Cordelia tried to get her wrist free but he kept a tight grip on it. 'Because you're married!'

'You mean because Sugin told you I was married.'

Cordelia stopped struggling and stared at him. 'What do you mean? She showed me a photograph of you and your wife.'

Marcus's mouth drew into a thin line. 'Of my ex-wife. We were divorced over a year ago.'

'Divorced?'

'Yes.'

Cordelia gazed at him, her head whirling. She moved her hand and this time he released it. Then she turned on her heel and began to hurry back towards the house.

'Where are you going?'

'I told you, back to England.'

In two strides he caught her up and placed himself in front of her. 'But why? After what I've told you?'

'Because it doesn't make any difference. You weren't honest with me.' Her voice broke. 'I thought that everything between us was open and wonderful. That we had no secrets from one another. You—you taught me not to be shy or inhibited, and I held nothing back from you. While all the time you were . . .'

'Listen, Cordelia.' Marcus took hold of her shoulders and spoke urgently. 'What we had was so perfect that I didn't want to spoil it. I wanted it to go on that way for as long as possible. Okay, maybe it was selfish of me, but I'd been through such hell, and we were so perfect together that . . .'

'Stop it!' Tears running down her face, Cordelia tried to hit out at him. 'I don't want to hear any more. I don't believe a word of it. I bet all the time we were making love you were comparing me to her.' She sobbed and struggled futilely against his imprisoning hands. 'Is she better in bed than I am—is she?'

'Oh, my love. My sweet, darling idiot!' Marcus tried to take her in his arms, but she wouldn't let him.

'Don't call me that. You don't love me. You've never said you love me.'

'That isn't true. I've told you many times.'

Cordelia stopped struggling and glared at him. 'Only—only when we were having sex. And that doesn't count.'

An amused look came into his grey-blue eyes. 'Is that what you think? You couldn't be more wrong.' Putting a hand on either side of her tear-stained face, he said steadily and firmly, 'I love you, Cordelia, with all my heart. I want to marry you and have from the first night we spent together. I admit that at first I wasn't sure that I wanted to marry again, because you were so young, and because having failed once there's always the fear that you might fail again. But I loved and wanted you so much that I had to take you, and then I found that we had something very special going for us, something I didn't want to spoil. Which is why I held back telling you.'

'Oh, Marcus!' He felt her body tremble, and then she walked into his arms. 'You big fool! If you don't kiss me this minute I'll just go crazy!'

So he did, with a passion that left her in no doubt of his feelings.

Some time later, when he had kissed away her tears and brought a flush to her cheeks again, Marcus sat on the grass with his back against the trunk of a tree and pulled her down on to his lap.

'Tell me about your wife,' Cordelia said softly. 'Just this once, and I'll never ask again.'

He shrugged. 'It's the usual story. We got married when we were far too young and grew apart. I'd just left university and was working in the kind of job that had good career prospects and a strong social life. But then I gave it up to write and she didn't like that, or the loss in money. There were rows. She wouldn't go out to work and made it difficult for me to work at home. We parted and then had a reconciliation after I had a couple of best-sellers. But she wouldn't come abroad with me when I wanted to do research and was always accepting invitations for me to give lectures or attend literary parties when all I wanted to do was write. So we split again and lived apart for two years so that we could qualify for a divorce—which is one of the reasons I came here.' A dark, brooding look came into his eyes and his arms tightened around her. 'The break-up of a marriage is a kind of hell of its own. You come out of it feeling old and battered and that nothing will ever be really good again. But then,' he added softly, his hand in her curls, 'a girl comes along with the sun in her smile and in her hair, and suddenly you come alive again.'

Cordelia put up a finger to smooth the lines

around his mouth and saw the shadows of remembered pain in his eyes. 'I'm sorry I ran away,' she said softly. 'But when you're very much in love you don't always think rationally and you're—you're very vulnerable.'

'Do you think I don't know?'

'Oh, Marcus!' Her arms went round his neck and they kissed lingeringly. Something brushed against her arm and Cordelia glanced up, then she gave a laugh of pure happiness. 'Hey, do you see which tree we're sitting under?'

Following her gaze, Marcus looked upwards and saw the white blossoms of the frangipani glowing like milk-white pearls in the sun. He grinned. 'And do you realise just how long it's been since . . .'

'Oh, yes,' Cordelia assured him feelingly. 'I most certainly do!'

'So what, woman, do you intend to do about it?'

She smiled at him, her eyes alight with love and happiness. 'What do you suggest?' He pulled her closer and whispered in her ear. Cordelia's eyebrows rose. 'Here? Now?'

'What's wrong with here and now?'

'Nothing. Nothing in the world.' And she gave herself happily to his embrace.

A WORD ABOUT THE AUTHOR

Sally Wentworth has spent most of her life in Hertfordshire, a rural county just north of the sprawling outskirts of London, England. She grew up in a village where everyone knew everyone else; a walk to the local shops could take two or three hours because one met so many people to chat with on the way.

Though she is basically a country person, it was in London, while working for a newspaper near bustling Fleet Street, that Sally met her husband-to-be. They honeymooned in romantic Paris and took an apartment in London at the beginning of their marriage, but they soon found themselves back where Sally's heart belonged—in Hertfordshire.

After her son was born, Sally began taking evening classes in creative writing. When her husband took on extra evening work, she found that the long quiet hours begged to be filled, and fill them she did — writing her first romance novel, *Island Masquerade* (Romance #2155) published in 1978.

She has written more than twenty books since then, and though her stories are set in fascinating foreign locales, she herself would not trade her home in the English countryside for anyplace else in the world.